Raves For the Work of
LAWRENCE BLOCK!

"Wonderful."
> —*USA Today*

"Addictive."
> —*Entertainment Weekly*

"Reads like it's been jolted by factory-fresh defibrillator pads."
> —*Time*

"A first-rate writer."
> —*Chicago Sun-Times*

"Block grabs you…and never lets go."
> —*Elmore Leonard*

"[The] one writer of mystery and detective fiction who comes close to replacing the irreplaceable John D. MacDonald."
> —*Stephen King*

"The suspense mounts and mounts and mounts…very superior."
> —*James M. Cain*

"The narrative is layered with detail, the action is handled with Block's distinctive clarity of style and the ending is a stunning tour de force."
> —*New York Times*

El Paso was a daylight town, quiet at night, and he walked the streets alone without seeing a single person. He was used to the night, and to silent walks down silent streets. In Tulsa, before the killing, before the little girl who had been so foolish as to ask him the time, he had been essentially a creature of the night. A quiet man. He had no friends in Tulsa. He spoke to no one and no one spoke to him.

Weaver had been a nobody in Tulsa, a man who had never done a thing. Now, walking through El Paso by night, he was at least a somebody for once. He had done something. The something was a horrible thing, but he had done it, and they had put his picture in the newspapers and had broadcast his name over the radio. They called him Dracula, and they called him the Cannibal Killer, but now, for the first time, they knew who he was.

Better to be loathed as a fiend than to be thoroughly ignored, better to be hated than not to be known at all. One act of horror had given direction to his life, had elevated him from nobody to somebody.

He went on walking. He walked surely now, his stride powerful, his arms swinging easily at his side. He was the Angel of Death, he thought. His life had a mission, a strange and terrifying sense of purpose.

He thought of that little girl in Tulsa. Before, that girl had seemed to have been a dreadful mistake, an end. But she was not an end at all. She was a beginning. She was the first person he had killed.

She would not be the last…

BORDERLINE

by **Lawrence Block**

A HARD CASE CRIME NOVEL

A HARD CASE CRIME BOOK
(HCC-115)
First Hard Case Crime edition: May 2014

Published by

Titan Books
A division of Titan Publishing Group Ltd
144 Southwark Street
London SE1 0UP

in collaboration with Winterfall LLC

Paperback Edition ISBN 978-1-78116-777-9
Hardcover Edition ISBN 978-1-78329-057-4
E-book ISBN 978-1-78116-778-6

Design direction by Max Phillips
www.maxphillips.net

Typeset by Swordsmith Productions

The name "Hard Case Crime" and the Hard Case Crime logo are trademarks of Winterfall LLC. Hard Case Crime books are selected and edited by Charles Ardai.

Printed in the United States of America

Visit us on the web at www.HardCaseCrime.com

BORDERLINE

CHAPTER ONE

Marty let up on the gas about fifty yards from the Customs shed. He put the clutch on the floor, ground the gears slightly, dropping the big Olds into second. Then his foot eased down on the brake and the car pulled up where it was supposed to. He rolled down his window and let his face relax into an automatic smile.

The guy on duty was a Texas redneck with a hawk nose and a pronounced Adam's apple. He grinned in recognition. "Anything to declare?"

"There's two cases of tequila in the trunk," Marty said. "And a hundred pounds of marijuana under the back seat. That's about it."

"Well, hell," the Customs man said. "Just so you ain't bringing back a dose or nothing. Go on."

The Customs shed was just an extra checkpoint, and the men on duty there didn't knock themselves out. There are, actually, two borders between the United States and Mexico. The official border is easily passable, and no passports or cards of identification are required. The working border is about sixty miles within Mexico, and that is where tourist cards are required and the Customs check is fairly rigorous. The reason for all this is a simple one. The border towns—Juarez and Tijuana and Nueva Laredo and Matamoros—thrive on American commerce. They operate under Mexican law and Mexican laissez-faire, yet they are easily accessible without a scrutinization or a host of red tape.

Marty smiled a final smile at the redneck, dropped the Olds

down into first, gunned the motor and popped the clutch. The Olds shot forward, six years old and still the fastest piece of iron on the road. Marty was in Texas now. El Paso. Ciudad Juarez was behind him, behind the Customs shed, on the other side of the border.

He drove along Crescent, took a left at Brantwood, turned right again on Coronado Avenue. He pulled up alongside a parking meter, got out of the car. Someone had left five minutes on the meter for him. But it would take more than five minutes to eat, even in a greasy spoon. Hell, it took five minutes before coffee got cool enough for him to drink it. He dug a nickel out of a pocket of his gray gabardine slacks, stuck it into the meter's hungry mouth, and crossed the street to the diner.

It had Formica counters, bare hanging light bulbs, a floor of cracked linoleum. A pair of truckers sat at the far end of the counter. One of them, the heavier one, was joking with the waitress. She had big breasts and a pair of washed-out eyes, and she laughed at everything the trucker said. The other trucker wasn't saying anything. He had his eyes on the girl's breasts, and you could read his thoughts without half-trying.

Otherwise, the place was empty. Marty found a stool at the other end of the counter from the truckers. He reached into his shirt pocket, pulled out a pack of Luckies with two bent cigarettes left in it. He selected one, straightened it out, lodged it between his lips. He left the cigarette pack on the counter and dug a Zippo lighter out of his back pocket. The chrome plating had worn off the lighter. It was a few years older than the Olds parked outside, and, like the Olds, it still worked perfectly. He thumbed the wheel and lit the cigarette. He inhaled, held the strong smoke in his lungs for a few seconds, then blew it at the ceiling.

By this time the waitress realized he was alive. She left the truckers reluctantly, scampered over to Marty. "Morning," she said. "The usual?"

"Fine, Betty."

She smiled when he called her by name. That was silly—everybody called her by name, because her name was embroidered on her white uniform just above her left breast, which was where everybody looked sooner or later. She went over to the window and told the cook she wanted ham and eggs, with the eggs sunny side up. She came back to Marty and leaned on the counter with her elbows. Her mouth was curved in a smile, and her breasts hung over the counter like ripe fruit from a tree.

"You weren't here yesterday," she said.

"I was across the border. In Juarez."

"All day?"

"All day and all night."

She wrinkled her nose at him. "You're a bad boy," she said playfully. "Those Mexican girls can give you a disease."

"I wasn't with a girl."

"Then why stay all night? You coulda driven back and slept at your own place. Why stay over?"

"I had business," he said. He wished she would shut up. Usually she made small talk without making a pest of herself. But right now she was getting on his nerves. She was asking questions, and he didn't feel like being grilled. He felt like eating a plate of ham and eggs and drinking a cup of coffee.

"Coffee," he said. "Want to bring it now?"

"Oh, sure. Just a minute."

She went to the coffee urn and drew a mugful for him. She set it on a saucer, put the saucer in front of him. "Black," she said. "No cream and no sugar. Right?"

"You should know."

She was leaning forward now, again. He stirred his coffee with his spoon and tried not to look at her breasts. He couldn't help it. They were hanging there, ripe fruit for plucking, and they were big and round, and they looked soft and touchable and—

Jesus, he thought, maybe I should have found a Mex girl, got some of it out of my system. Three bucks for a nice hot Mex girl, a wham and a bam and a thank you, Ma'am. But Betty had good breasts, big ones, and she stuck them out at you and you could see their outlines clearly through the uniform, could see the way they twisted the blouse of the uniform slightly out of shape. And she probably wasn't even wearing a bra; the way she was leaning, the way the breasts looked, and, oh, man!

"Betty," the trucker said, "c'mere."

"He's calling you," Marty said.

"He can go to hell," she said. "Those truck drivers. All they want to do is joke dirty and talk dirty and maybe touch you and proposition you. To hell with him."

"And you don't want to be touched."

"Well," she said.

He looked at her. There was a smile on her lips. She stuck out her tongue, licked her lips like a tiger after a good meal. Her eyes were not so washed-out now. They were a brighter blue, and her hair was spun gold, and her lips warm coral.

"Sometimes I want to be touched," she said. "It depends who's doing the touching. It makes a difference."

The cook broke things up by ringing a little bell. Betty turned at the sound and Marty watched her walk to the window for his ham and eggs. The skirt of her uniform hugged her buttocks, and they swayed as she walked.

She's doing that on purpose, he thought. Swinging the rump for the same reason she sticks the boobs out.

She brought him his food. The yellow yolks stood up like breasts on a girl, he thought. And he wished he could stop thinking about girls in general and breasts in particular. He took his silverware, wiped it with a paper napkin, attacked the food. Betty stood there and watched him eat. It was annoying. He looked up at her, letting part of the annoyance show in his eyes, and she turned away and walked back to the two truckers. They wanted more coffee, and they wanted to talk to Betty.

He was hungry and he ate in a hurry. The coffee was barely warm when he got around to it, and that was the way he liked it. Some men damn near burned their mouths with coffee. He liked it warm, but not hot. That way you got the flavor of it.

He needed a second cup of coffee. He cleared his throat, once, and Betty turned away from the truckers and hurried after him. She filled his cup and gave it back to him, her eyes wide, warm.

"You were in Juarez on business," she said.

"Yeah."

"What kind of business?"

He thought of telling her to go to hell. "Private business," he said.

"You in business for yourself?"

He permitted himself to smile. "You could call it that."

"What kind of business? Monkey business? Sometimes that's the best kind, you know."

He took his last cigarette from the pack on the counter. He spun the wheel of the Zippo, lit the cigarette. "I'm a gambler," he said. "I went to Juarez to play poker. I played until the game broke up. Then I came back to El Paso."

"You're a gambler?"

"Yeah."

"You stayed there all that time for a poker game?"

He didn't answer. He remembered the basement room at Navarro's house, air-conditioned, plush chairs, a green-shaded light hanging from the ceiling. No clock on the wall. Chips on the table, chips that went back and forth. Now it was Friday morning. Around ten Wednesday night he had sat down at the table with five hundred dollars worth of chips. Two hours ago he had cashed in twenty-eight hundred dollars. Now it was in a money belt around his waist. He remembered hand after hand after hand, voices that said only the words needed to bet and raise and call and fold.

"I stayed there all that time," he said. "For a poker game."

"You win?"

"Yeah."

"You usually win?"

"I'm a gambler," he said, annoyed again, annoyed with the silly words and the big breasts and the thorough lack of subtlety. "Of course I usually win. Otherwise I'd do something else for a living."

She digested this. He stood up, tired of the girl, tired of the diner, tired of the clothes he'd been wearing since Wednesday. He dug into a pants pocket, found a loose single to cover the food and coffee. He added a quarter for the girl.

"You're a gambler," she said.

He thought that if she leaned over any further, she was going to drill boob-shaped holes in the counter's Formica top. He picked up his cigarette from the little glass ashtray and put it between his lips.

"You could gamble on me," she said. "You could try your luck."

He reached out a hand and touched her breast with it. The flesh was firm, unyielding. He wanted to squeeze, to caress it.

Instead, he let go.

"I'm a gambler," he said. "But I never play sure things."

He turned around and left the diner. She yelled something dirty after him, something dirty enough to make the truckers spin on their stools and laugh. Outside, he crossed the street to the Olds, opened the door and got behind the wheel. He put his key in the ignition, started the car, pulled away from the curb.

It was hot, he thought. Not even eleven in the morning and hot as hell already. By afternoon, when the sun really got warmed up, it was going to be horrible.

He drove home.

Meg Rector slept until noon. Sleeping was easy. The hotel was expensive and the air-conditioning worked the way it was supposed to. The bed she slept in had a firm mattress. The sheets were good percale, and they were perfectly clean. She'd had half a pint of Beefeater gin before she went to bed, not enough to leave her hung over in the morning, just enough to make deep sleep come in a hurry.

At noon she awoke. For a moment there was a nebulous where-am-I feeling, the unfamiliar sensation that comes with waking in a strange bed in a strange room in an unfamiliar city. This didn't stay long. She stretched and shook her head and remembered where she was.

The Hotel Warwick, in El Paso. A room on the tenth and top floor with a view of the city, for what it was worth. Alone, of course. Alone, and twenty-six years old, and divorced, and bored. And, now, awake. She got up from the bed, her hair black and loose and long, trailing down over bare shoulders that were just barely tanned. She was wearing a nightgown sheer and black, and she looked down at it and laughed humorlessly. You don't have to wear a nightgown anymore, she told herself. You're not married anymore. You can sleep naked, the way you used to.

She stepped out of the nightgown, walked to the closet, hung the gown on a wire hanger. Then she changed her mind, took the nightgown from the hanger, balled it into a nylon ball and stuffed it into the wastebasket by the dresser. You can sleep naked, she told herself again. No more nightgowns. So why fill a closet with them?

Meg walked naked into the bathroom. Her toothbrush and a small tube of toothpaste were on the rim of the sink where she had left them before going to bed. She brushed her teeth, rinsed her mouth. She unwrapped a small cake of soap, turned on the stall shower, got into it. She lathered herself thoroughly, washed herself thoroughly, holding her head back to keep the water away from her hair. She got out of the shower, dried off with a towel, went back to the bed and sat on its edge.

El Paso, for God's sake. She remembered getting there, remembered first of all flying to Mexico City from Chicago just a week ago, remembered spending a week at an expensive American hotel on Reforma while her divorce went through. It wasn't like being in Mexico. The whole street was for Americans, everybody spoke English, and it was like Miami or Vegas or Palm Springs, just another resort for Americans with too much money. She killed a week, talking to no one, staying in her room for hours on end and sipping Beefeater gin from a water tumbler. She ate all her meals in the hotel's dining room. Then the divorce was through. She wasn't married to Borden Rector any more, she was an emancipated woman, and there was no reason to stay in Mexico City anymore.

She would have had to wait eight hours for a nonstop plane back to Chicago. There was a flight leaving right away, stopping at El Paso and Kansas City before it got to Chicago. She took it, using the return half of the round-trip ticket that Borden Rector's attorney had given to her along with a sheaf of forms and a bundle of expense money.

At El Paso she got out of the plane, managed to get her luggage back even though it was checked through to Chicago. She didn't know anybody in El Paso, and didn't want to. Nothing fascinated her about El Paso. But she had realized, while the big plane was in the air, that she had no desire at all to return to Chicago. And flying was dull, monotonous.

So here she was, in El Paso.

She stood up. Her purse was in the dresser's top drawer. She found her cigarette case in it, took out a cigarette, lit it and smoked. She caught a glimpse of herself in the mirror on the closet door, stopped and regarded herself thoughtfully. She saw the long black hair that had remained miraculously dry in the shower, saw the tall body with the full curves and the trim waist and the full, flaring hips. Her arms and legs and face were slightly tanned, but the rest of her body was a very pale white, with the white breasts almost shocking with their crimson tips.

She looked at herself. *Nude Smoking a Cigarette* she titled the picture. She laughed again, an audible laugh, a mirthless laugh. She ground out the cigarette in an ashtray and put clothes on.

Downstairs, in the lobby, she walked to the room clerk's desk and coughed until the little round-shouldered clerk scurried over to her.

"Where's a decent restaurant?"

"Just around the corner," he told her. "You go out that door—" he pointed "—and turn right, and walk to the corner, that's Carleton Boulevard and you turn right again. Giardi's Restaurant is just four doors from the corner."

"Italian food?"

"Italian and American. It's very good there."

His brother probably owned it, she decided. But he didn't look very Italian. Maybe his brother-in-law owned it. Or maybe his brother had purchased it from Giardi, or—

The clerk was still waiting patiently. "Listen," she said, "what the hell do you do in this town?"

The clerk looked puzzled. He was wearing glasses, thick glasses, and they made his eyes seem enormous.

He said, "Do?"

"For excitement. What goes on?"

The clerk took a short breath, thought, expelled the breath. "Why, there are movie theaters," he said. "And night clubs, of course. There's a listing of entertainment in the daily newspaper, the *El Paso Sun*. And then there is Juarez, of course."

"Across the border?"

"Yes. It's a…a border town. Not a very decent sort of place, I'm afraid, but quite a few persons go there for…for amusement. But it depends what sort of excitement—"

She told him to forget it. She turned around, went out the door he had pointed to, walked to Carleton Boulevard and found Giardi's. The food was better than she had expected. She asked for a breakfast menu, found out they had stopped serving breakfast two hours ago, and stopped the waiter in mid-sentence when he started to offer to get her an omelet, maybe, or some wheat cakes, or—

She had a plate of spaghetti with chicken livers and a bottle of red wine. She had never cared much for breakfast food, hated eggs and couldn't stomach cereal. But Borden liked breakfast. Every day, for four years, Borden liked breakfast.

Four years of Borden. Four years of marriage, four years that added up to fourteen or fifteen hundred days, and every day the same, except that each was a little more horribly monotonous than the last. Four years of wearing a nightgown to bed because Borden thought it was indecent to sleep in the raw. Four years of making love briefly, and rarely; four years of on-again off-again, with Borden finished and ready to sleep just as she started to get interested in the game.

A year, perhaps, of running to the bathroom and finishing the job herself. Then three years of not bothering, because Borden had not even managed to arouse her. Three years of cheating now and then; not out of need as much as out of boredom. Four years of dullness and drabness, of having money without enjoying it, of living, damn it to hell, with Borden.

For excitement, she had told the clerk. What did it mean? God, how did she know what it meant? Maybe it meant getting laid or getting drunk or shooting dice or taking dope or driving in a fast car. She hadn't seen any excitement in too long. She hardly remembered what it was like.

She had a cup of coffee and smoked a cigarette with it. El Paso, she thought. And Juarez. Somewhere in one town or the other, there was going to be a little excitement. Somewhere in Texas or Mexico there was going to be a reprieve from the boredom, a respite from the monotony. Call it excitement, or call it something else. It hardly mattered.

She paid the tab, tipped the waiter. Outside it was hotter than hell—that was the trouble with air-conditioning; you couldn't stand it when you were out in the open again. She headed automatically for the Warwick, then stopped halfway there, turned on her heel and headed off in the opposite direction. That wasn't what she wanted. She'd had her fill in Mexico City in the hotel on Reforma. Sit in the room, drink Beefeater, go out for dinner, go back to the room and drink some more. No, thank you. That was no way to find excitement.

She stayed on Carleton Boulevard until she found a cocktail lounge that looked inviting. It was air-conditioned, it had low ceilings and dim lighting, and it looked expensive enough to keep the riff-raff out.

She went inside. She took a table on the side, asked the waiter for Beefeater and ice. Then she waited for something to happen.

Lily was on the road for twenty minutes before a car stopped. It was a flat, empty stretch of road, a chunk of Route 49 halfway between Dallas and El Paso. Desert country, dry and desolate. Her last ride had dropped her there, and she was beginning to wonder if maybe she hadn't made a mistake taking the last ride. The driver had dropped her in this godforsaken middle of nowhere, said he was turning off another mile down the road. Maybe she should have waited for a ride clear through to El Paso.

She was a small girl, just a few inches above five feet. She was seventeen. Her face looked about two years younger than that until you saw her eyes, which looked twenty-five. Her figure was petite but perfect. Chunky breasts pushed out the front of the short-sleeved boy's shirt she wore, and neatly rounded hips filled the khaki slacks. On her feet she wore simple leather sandals that had been hand-made by a Negro leatherworker in San Francisco's North Beach area. The sandals were very comfortable.

North Beach, and S.F. She hadn't started out there. She was a Denver girl who ran away from home three weeks after her sixteenth birthday, and S.F. was a natural place to stop running, and the Beach was a natural spot to grab for a home. She liked the area. She spent a year there, living here now and there now, meeting people and doing things. Her parents never found her. Maybe they didn't look.

A year in S.F. A year that didn't age her face a day, but that turned her eyes from child's eyes to woman's eyes. A year that made her rock-hard inside. A year that taught her many things.

Then she was hooked up with Frank, who was tight with Spider Graham. And then one day S.F. was too hot for the Spider. Spider, thin and tight-lipped and nervous, had robbed a liquor store with a toy gun. The rollers had a make on him and the Spider had to run. Frank was his friend, so Frank went with him. She was Frank's steady lay, so she went too.

They stole plates from a Cadillac and slapped the plates on a Ford and stole the Ford. They drove the hell out of the car, running south, skirting L.A., cutting out through Death Valley and across Arizona. The car died somewhere in the middle of New Mexico and they stole a Chevy off the streets of a sleeping town and pushed east again. They parked the stolen Chevy in a lot in Dallas and the Spider dropped the parking check down a sewer. They all laughed like hell and tried to figure out something to do in Dallas, some way to put a few dollars together.

Spider had an idea. They had a commodity named Lily Daniels. They would trade Lily in for money. Rather, they would rent her out, and live off the proceeds.

Frank thought it was a great idea.

Lily thought it stank. She was a few million miles from virginity but she wasn't a whore. She would give for a guy because she liked him, or she would give for a guy because she was hot to go, or she would give for a guy because maybe it would be a minor gas. She never gave for money. She didn't have eyes for the notion.

She didn't have any choice, either. Spider went out to pimp, and he came back with a drunk Texan fifty years old and clumsy as hell. And slung like a bull. They put the Texan in the room with her and she tried to tell him it was a mistake.

He ripped off her blouse, grabbed her breasts in his hands and squeezed them until they ached.

"I paid a hundred dollars for you, dolly," he said. "I paid the money to that nervous kid with the skinny lips. You don't go and tell me now it was a mistake. I don't make mistakes, not for no hundred dollars."

"Please—"

He slapped her face. He hit her in the stomach, and her hands went out for his face, to claw him. He brushed her hands away casually, hit her on the top of the head.

She started to fall, and he kicked her in the breast. He was wearing heavy boots and the pain was unbelievable. She thought she was going to die. "You want more, dolly?"

"No," she said. "I'll do it."

She took off her clothes and got on the bed. He took her with no preliminaries; evidently the beating had aroused him if not her. He plunged into her, and he was far too large and hurt her far too much. And it all lasted far too long. When it was over she was horribly sore, and sick to her stomach.

He left the bed, sat down in a chair. She reached for her clothes and he said, "Not yet, dolly."

She didn't understand.

"I paid that skinny fellow a hundred dollars," he said. "I got something more coming for my hundred dollars. The last was pleasant, but I got more coming."

"What?"

He told her, explicitly.

She stood in front of him, her eyes wide. "He told you I'd do that? Spider said I'd do it?"

"Said you loved to do it," the Texan said. "Me, I don't care whether you love it or not. You just do it or I'll beat you half dead."

He would, she thought dully. He would kill her. She did not want to be beaten. She still ached badly and she did not want any more pain.

She sank to her knees before him. He stroked her hair, like a father patting his daughter on the head, and he told her she was a sweet little dolly. And she did everything he wanted her to do.

Afterward, she looked for Spider and Frank. She couldn't find them and they did not come back to the room. They had left Dallas, as far as she could tell, and they probably would not be back. Hell, they definitely would not be back. And she didn't have a penny.

That was two days ago. She'd managed to eat, managed to talk people into buying food for her. And now she was on the road to El Paso, halfway there on Route 49. She didn't know why she was going to El Paso. But from El Paso she could go to Mexico and she knew people in Mexico, people who'd been her friends in S.F.

She stood on the road for twenty minutes before the car stopped.

The car was a big Buick, air-conditioned, with power windows and power doors and power brakes and power steering and power everything. The driver was a dark man in a business suit. He had deep eyes and thinning hair. She guessed his age at forty-five.

He leaned across the seat and pressed a button. The window went down and he looked through it at Lily. He asked her where she was headed. She told him she was going to El Paso.

"Hop in," he said. "I'll run you there."

She sat beside him and he pulled away again, his foot heavy on the accelerator. She pressed the button to close the window because the car was air-conditioned. It was a pleasure to get out of the heat, she thought. And the Buick was a fast car. They would be in El Paso in no time at all.

They drove two miles in silence. Then he asked her her name, and where she was going. She made up a name to tell him and said she was visiting relatives. He asked her how come she was hitchhiking and she told him she wanted to save money.

"Spend all your money on pretty clothes?"

She was wearing khakis and a shirt that was dirty now. She had no suitcase.

"I didn't have any money," she said.

"I see."

Two miles further on down the road he dropped a hand to her thigh. She looked down at the hand. It looked like a separate entity, a living creature poised on her thigh. He moved the hand higher, along the inside of her thigh, and she sighed.

"Pull over," she said.

"You mad, honey? I just—"

"Pull over." she said, tired now. "I want a ride to El Paso. You want a ride too, I guess. I guess we'll both have one."

He pulled the car off the road and killed the ignition. They went from the front seat to the back seat, and he opened her shirt and took off her pants. She was still a little sore from the man in the hotel room but it wasn't too bad.

When it was over he was breathing hard, his face covered with sweat. It seemed odd to her that a man could sweat so much in an air-conditioned car. He was exhausted, and wordless, while she herself was completely unmoved. It was as though he had not touched her at all. He had used her body, had enjoyed the outer shell, but he had not come close to the person who was Lily Daniels.

"You're a real woman," he told her. "I hope you don't think I would have forced you or anything. I'd of driven you to Paso anyway, even if you didn't want to do anything."

"I know," she said.

"But you wanted it too," he said. "You had yourself a fine time. I could tell, all right. I know when a woman likes it."

If he wanted to think so, that was fine with her. She put her clothes on, combed her hair back. They returned to the front seat and he started the motor, headed for El Paso again. He drove very fast this time. She watched the speedometer and it passed a hundred frequently.

She saw the tan road rushing toward them in a never-ending stream, everything blurred from the great speed at which they were traveling.

But it was as if they weren't traveling—so fast was the speed. It was if they were soaring through space somewhere.

Then they would hit a bump, or a rut in the road, and the car would rock slightly and she would be brought back to the reality that they were on the ground and not in the air—on the ground and traveling a hundred miles an hour.

She looked out the side window but the poles and cacti passed by the window so fast that she could not even tell they were there. Only when she looked hundreds of yards past the road could she see anything clearly—and then her pupils had to jerk rapidly across her eyes to see even that.

She turned her head and glanced out the rear window but she could see nothing but a mad swirl of dust.

It was far to El Paso, that she knew although she didn't know just how far it was. Yet suddenly they were passing an occasional home and he let up on the gas. It seemed like they weren't even moving now and she glanced down at the speedometer. They were going sixty!

Then as they began to reach the outskirts of El Paso he let

up on the gas even more and the speedometer dropped to forty.

In El Paso, at a traffic light, he took two ten-dollar bills from his wallet and handed them to her. He was shy about it, telling her he wanted her to have a good meal and buy a pretty dress. She thanked him and got out of the car.

El Paso, she said to herself. Now what?

Just what could she do here?

She didn't know.

Yet she had gotten this far without ever knowing what she was going to do from one minute to the next.

Somehow she'd gotten this far all right. All right, once she had gotten away from Frank and Spider. Or they had gotten away from her.

Whichever way it was didn't matter. Just the fact that she was no longer with them was all that mattered.

No matter what happened to her now—it couldn't be worse than what had happened to her in that hotel room. Worse than that Texan had done to her.

She could still feel the pain.

In spite of the comfortable car ride.

In spite of the cool air-conditioning.

In spite of the two days that had passed, and the hundreds of miles she'd put between herself and that room. In spite of it all, the pain was still there.

Aching.

Throbbing.

Her thigh muscles so sore, she had trouble walking.

And inside of her—the pain extended deep inside her, and the tiny finger-edges of it extended themselves to all parts of her body.

She had to get out of El Paso, and into Mexico. But first she had to get washed and rested, and get some food in her empty stomach.

But how?

Then she slowly remembered the bills she held in her hand. She looked at them.

Twenty dollars, twenty dollars, twenty dollars, her mind repeated and she smiled to herself.

CHAPTER TWO

The hotel where Weaver was staying was a far cry from the Warwick. This one was called Cappy's Hotel, and it was on Hinesdale at the corner of Eighteenth. A skid row dump, no air-conditioning and plenty of insects. There was a fan that hung from the ceiling. Weaver lay on his back on a sagging army cot and the fan blew hot air at him. He was lying in a pool formed of his own sweat. The sweat had been caused half by the heat and half by his fear. Weaver was afraid.

His full name was Michael Patrick Weaver. His friends might have called him Mike or Mickey or Mick or M.P. It was a moot point, for Weaver had no friends. He was short and wiry and ugly, with a little pimple of a nose and no chin at all. His eyes were pig eyes, beady pig eyes, and his forehead was low enough to justify Lombroso's theories about the physiology of the criminal type. His hair was black and coarse with no curl to it. He wore it combed down across his forehead, an uncon-scious imitation of Hitler, and this only lowered his forehead that much more. His teeth were bad. They were yellow, pocked with cavities, and two of the incisors were chipped. He was ugly from top to bottom, and his fear made him even uglier.

They were going to kill him. He thought about this, and shivered. They were going to catch him, first, and then they were going to cart him back to Tulsa. Then the police would give him a beating.

He knew all about police beatings. He'd had one once, when that big raw-boned cop had caught him having a look in a window. There had been a broad in the window, and the broad had had her clothes off, and Weaver had been having a look. He had stared at her, the feverish excitement mounting within him, the passion building. He hadn't hurt the broad. He had only stared at her breasts and genitals, had let his mind construct harmless fantasies that hadn't hurt the broad a bit.

But the cop saw him, and grabbed him, and dragged him down to the police station. They booked him as a Peeping Tom and they beat the hell out of him. He remembered the big cop working on his face, slapping backhand and forehand, until he couldn't see straight. He remembered a shorter cop with a rubber truncheon. They had tough cops in Tulsa.

And that was just for watching, just for being a harmless Peeping Tom. That had gotten him a beating and a fingerprinting and a suspended sentence. This thing, now, was different. This thing was going to get him electrocuted. This thing would get him a very bad beating, three times as bad as the time when he looked at the broad. And after they beat him there would be a trial, and he would be found guilty, and then they would strap him in a chair and throw a switch.

He would smell his own flesh burning as the current jolted through his body, Then he would be dead, and it would be over.

Forever.

He shivered, a weird action in the intense heat. He remembered now, remembered the thing he had done. His breathing grew heavy as the scene flashed through his mind again:

A night, and a girl.

The girl was thirteen years old. He didn't know this then but found it out later in the newspaper stories. The girl was thirteen years old, and the girl had soft pale green eyes and the budding breasts of a precocious adolescent. Brown hair, soft brown hair that would be very soft to touch. Legs that were starting to come into their own, a little awkward still, a

slight bit bony, but beginning to fill out. A mouth with no lipstick on it.

She shouldn't have been out that late. It was after midnight,
Saturday night, and Weaver was on his way home from the
movies. They had a pair of horror movies that night, one about
a vampire who drank the blood of women, one about a man
who could transform himself into a black panther and leap from
trees upon passing girls.

The movies had excited Weaver. He had imagined himself as
the vampire in one beautiful sequence where they had shown
the vampire, his fangs in the neck of a terror-stricken blonde.
Weaver remembered the shrill screams of the blonde, remembered how the camera had shown the tops of her creamy
breasts, how the vampire had sucked her blood and left her
dead. In the other movie he had mentally changed placed with
the black panther. When the animal dropped from a high limb
upon the back of a youthful brunette—this girl, too, providen-
tially equipped with a low-cut gown that exposed her breasts—
Weaver's excitement had been almost too much to bear. The
beast's talons clawed the girl's shoulders and Weaver wanted to
scream with passion. And now he was on his way home. The
passion was bottled up inside; when he reached his small furnished room on Tulsa's north side, he would relive the two movies
and relieve his frustrations the only way he knew. For now, he
was just walking. Walking alone, through dark streets.

And then he saw the girl. She was walking toward him, and
he looked at the fluffy brown hair that looked so soft. He saw
her waist and thought that he could span it with his hands. He
saw her breasts, and he saw the promise her loins held. He saw
her throat, an ivory column, and he recalled the teeth of the
vampire in the throat of the blonde.

Even then he might have done nothing, might merely have

added her to his masturbatory fantasy that night. But she spoke to him. She walked right up to him and asked him what time it was.

He didn't own a watch. He told her it was late. His voice had an odd quality to it, a metallic whine.

"Oh, gosh," she said. "I should of been home hours ago. I went to this movie, see, with Elvis in it, and it was so good I saw it through three times. My Ma's gonna skin me alive, but it was some picture. Don't you just love Elvis?"

Those were the last words the girl ever spoke.

The streets were dark and empty. Weaver grabbed her, one hand over her mouth, the other on her shoulder. There was no convenient alleyway but a darkened storefront was a handy substitute. He got her into the storefront, his arms strong with muscle and desperation. He released her for a moment, and her mouth opened for a scream. He hit her in the mouth with his closed fist. He knocked out three of her front teeth.

She was wearing a plaid skirt and a pale yellow blouse. He tore the blouse open and buttons bounced crazily on the pavement. He cupped her breasts with his hands, squeezed, then tore her bra in two. The breasts sprang out with rosebud nipples at their tips.

He was the panther now. He slapped a hand over her bleeding mouth and banged her head against the pavement. He sprang at her, and his teeth found her breast, and his teeth closed in the grip of a vise. A black panther striking his prey—

The girl screamed against his hand. He bit her breasts, drew blood from the tender flesh. His hands tore her skirt upward, reduced her cheap white cotton panties to scattered remnants of cloth. He grabbed her with one hand and tugged at the tenderest part of her body, biting her breast flesh all the while with his chipped yellow teeth.

He fumbled with his own clothing. He undressed himself as much as was necessary and threw himself upon her. Whenever she tried to moan, he slapped her head against the pavement. He took her, forcing himself into her, and while he violated her his teeth found her throat.

He was the panther no longer. He was the vampire, now.

One of Tulsa's newspapers called him the Cannibal Killer. The other referred to him as Dracula. Both described how the girl's flesh had been literally eaten away in sections, how there were toothmarks in her throat, how the back of her head was a pulpy mess from the beating he had given her. Both reported quite honestly that she was very very dead, and that she had not died pleasantly at all.

He left fingerprints behind. His fingerprints were on record, from before, and the police knew who he was. He left Tulsa, running like a frightened rabbit rather than a lordly panther. He left on a Trailways bus and headed for Mexico. He had seen criminals run for Mexico to escape the law. It seemed as good a place to go as any. He ran like a rabbit, and he found a rabbit warren hotel in El Paso, and he was there now.

Because it was not so easy to run to Mexico. The men at the border had his picture and his description and his fingerprints, and they would be waiting for him to try to get across. As long as he stayed in Cappy's Hotel he was reasonably safe, at least until the police followed him to El Paso and made a door-to-door check for him. The minute he tried to cross the border, they would grab him.

He had already given up. He'd developed a fatalistic attitude about it all. Soon—in a week or two—he would run out of money. Soon he'd be a rabbit flushed from its burrow. Then they would catch him. And beat him. And strap him in the electric chair so that he could smell his own flesh burning.

Now it was only a matter of staying alive as long as he could, of living each day as it came and waiting for the police. He had been at Cappy's Hotel for almost a week. He stayed in his room as much as he could, leaving it only to eat at a lunch counter down the street or to buy comic books at a newsstand. The comic books were horror comics, the only kind he cared for. Right now there was a huge stack of them on the cigarette-scarred bureau. He had read them all twice through.

He stood up. There was a sink in the room, its porcelain bowl stained yellow where the water from each tap ran to the drain in the center. He ran water into the bowl, dipped a towel into it, and wiped the sweat from his ugly face. He got his hair wet and combed it down over his forehead, the way he liked it. He looked at himself for just a second in the cracked mirror over the bowl.

He had to go to the bathroom. His room was a cheap one, two bucks a day, and it did not have a private bathroom. He put on a shirt and walked out of his room, leaving the door ajar. He headed down the hallway.

The girl was leaving the bathroom just as he was approaching it. He looked at the girl. She looked at him, then averted her eyes. Women seldom looked at Weaver for any length of time. He was, really, very little to look at.

But the girl was fine to look at. She was short and slender, with breasts that pushed her shirt front out and hips that fitted her khaki pants snugly.

Weaver did not know that her name was Lily Daniels.

He knew only that she looked very much like another girl, a girl in Tulsa, a girl he had raped and tortured and killed. A little older, but similar, like she might have been the other girl's big sister. He turned to watch her continue on down the hall. She went into a room just next door to his, and he kept watching her until she had closed her door.

He went to the bathroom and used the toilet. He went back

to his own room, then, and closed the door and sat on the edge of the bed under the fan, which resumed blowing hot air upon him. He tried to sit still but it was impossible. He could not get the girl out of his mind, could not banish her image, could not stop his mind from inventing horrible things that he wanted to do to her. She was like the girl in Tulsa, and he had done terrible things to the girl in Tulsa.

He wondered what he was going to do Lily Daniels. Something awful, he thought. Something really terrible. The thought excited him.

Meg Rector was drunk, more or less. She hadn't planned it that way, not when she first entered the dimly lighted cocktail lounge. She'd planned on having a few drinks, and she'd planned on finding some excitement in one way or another, but she hadn't planned on getting drunk.

It had worked out that way. The excitement, nebulous enough in her own mind, had failed to materialize. The bar drew a quiet crowd—dark men in lightweight suits whom she somehow assumed to be gangsters, cool-eyed women in expensive gowns, upper-middle-class married couples having a quiet drink before dinner. There was soft music and subdued conversation. There was no excitement.

Meg stayed at her table. From time to time her glass was empty, and from time to time the waiter came and took away the empty, replacing it with fresh Beefeater and a pair of fresh ice cubes. She drank her drinks slowly enough, never getting high, never sinking into alcoholic depression, never even realizing the effect the liquor was having upon her.

A chemical and biological fact was responsible for the fact that she got drunk. The fact is this: the liver removes alcohol from the bloodstream at the rate of one ounce per hour. A man may drink one ounce of alcohol per hour for his entire lifetime and never become remotely drunk. But if he drinks more than an ounce per hour, and if he does this for a sufficient number of hours, he's going to fall under alcohol's influence. This is inevitable.

Meg averaged two drinks an hour, and each had a full jigger of 90-proof gin. A jigger is an ounce and a half, and 90-proof gin is forty-five percent alcohol, so with the aid of pencil and paper and patience one can easily determine that she was taking in one and one-third ounces of alcohol per hour. She had a head start, too, in the form of the bottle of chianti she had had at Giardi's.

By seven in the evening, then, she was drunk.

She stood up slowly but steadily, took a crisp dollar bill from her purse, folded it once and dropped it upon the table top for the waiter. She walked steadily out of the cocktail lounge to the street. At the doorway she braced herself for a rush of unbearable heat, since the cocktail lounge had been air-conditioned and since the street was not. She opened the door and stepped outside, and she was surprised to discover that the breeze which blew at her was pleasantly cool. El Paso evidently cooled off in the evenings, and for this she was thankful. Heat right now might knock her over. Hot air, after a plethora of gin, is a bad chaser.

She breathed deeply, filling her lungs with the breeze. She felt fine, she decided; not at all wobbly, not at all nauseous, not at all sober. It was a good feeling. If excitement was going to materialize, she was going to be able to accept it. She was in the right sort of mood. Not sick, not ready to fall on her face, and not sober.

At the corner she saw that she was still on Carleton Boulevard. So far the street had been good to her, having supplied her with good food at Giardi's and good gin at the cocktail lounge. She saw no valid reason to desert Carleton Boulevard. She crossed the street and stayed with Carleton, heading toward more bright lights.

The bright light section was the approach to the border. She saw small shops selling souvenirs of Mexico, which impressed her as odd items to purchase on the Texas side. Other shops offered to convert dollars to pesos. She still had Mexican money in her purse, money from Mexico City which she had never bothered to reconvert into dollars.

Now, evidently, she would have a chance to spend some of it, some of those one- and five- and ten-peso notes. A peso was around eight cents, she knew, and it was hard to think of a bill worth eight cents as being legal tender in anything but Monopoly. She stopped by a streetlight to take her wallet from her purse and go through the Mexican bills in one compartment. She had eighty-six pesos, or $6.88. She wondered what she could buy with eighty-six pesos. Not very much, she decided. But she knew they took American money in Juarez, just as they had in Mexico City.

They didn't even stop her at the Customs shed. She could understand that; the only thing you could smuggle profitably into Mexico was gold, and she could hardly carry gold in a handbag. Cars were a profitable smuggling item as well, since Mexico had a hundred percent import duty on them, but she was on foot. The Customs man smiled at her and motioned her on through. She took a few dozen steps and she was in Mexico again.

Ciudad Juarez, she said to herself. Big deal.

There were no cigarettes in her sterling silver cigarette case. She found her way to a stand that sold junk jewelry and souvenirs and cigars and tequila and, finally, cigarettes. She looked at the display and pointed to a pack labeled *Delicados*. A Mexican with a drooping moustache handed her the pack and she gave him a one-peso note. Surprisingly, he returned some Mexican coins in change. She looked at them oddly, wondering what they could give you that was change for eight cents. She dropped the coins in her purse, opened the pack of cigarettes and filled her cigarette case. She lit one, drew on it, inhaled. It tasted exactly like any American cigarette.

In flawless English, the Mexican asked her if she would like to buy a packet of filthy pictures.

Sober, she might have stalked away haughtily. Sober and still married to Borden Rector, she would certainly have done so. But she was drunk and divorced and hunting for excitement. While she could imagine more exciting fare than filthy photographs, she didn't want to miss any bets.

"Filthy pictures," she said. "How filthy?"

"Very filthy."

"What do they show?"

He told her, in perfect English, what the pictures showed. He would never have dreamed of using the equivalent Spanish words in a woman's presence, not even if the woman were a prostitute. That was an interesting thing about using a foreign language, Meg thought. You never quite realized how dirty the dirty words were.

"How much?"

"A dollar," he said.

She looked through her purse. "Ten pesos," she suggested.

It was a deal. The man would have taken five pesos, as it happened, but Meg was not particularly concerned about saving pesos. She gave him the bill, took a small manila envelope, and left the stand. She kept walking until she came to a public park with green benches. She found an unoccupied bench, sat down on it, and opened the manila envelope.

The photos were filthy, all right. She looked at each of the dozen in turn, and when she had finished she went through the batch again and devoted her attention to the more dramatic ones. There were five different characters in the set, two men and three women. One man was an American, probably a soldier boy having the time of his life on a furlough. The rest of the characters were all Mexican.

Two of the pictures showed the two men making love to one of the Mexican girls, a young one with bleached blonde hair and incredibly large breasts. Two more pictures showed the soldier, one shot involving two of the girls and the other all three. After a furlough like that one, Meg decided, the soldier would be able to live on memories for the rest of his hitch in the service.

Another picture had all five characters represented, and what they were doing seemed interesting as hell if slightly impossible. Meg spent a long time looking at that picture.

There were two pictures of girls only. These interested Meg, too—she had always wondered idly what it was that lesbians did, and now she knew. A picture was worth a few thousand words on the current rate of exchange. She now knew what they did, although she still wasn't sure whether it could be fun or not.

The rest of the pictures were one-man-and-one-woman stuff, exciting enough in their own right but overshadowed by the more involved and esoteric shots. Each picture, black and white and glossy, served to point up one fact which had already occurred to Meg. To wit—she needed a man.

She needed a man desperately. She was looking at one of the man-woman pictures, and the part of Meg's own body which corresponded to the area of the Mexican girl's body that the man was kissing—that part itched. Itched furiously and needed to be scratched.

She was still looking at the clever little picture, and still itching, and still needing a man, when she heard a voice at her elbow.

"Well, hello," the voice said. "What have you got there?"

She looked up at the man who had spoken. He was an American, dark-haired and broad-shouldered and tie-less. He was around thirty-five, Meg guessed. And good-looking. And fairly sure of himself, poised, easygoing.

"I've got filthy pictures here," she said. "Have a seat and have a look, friend."

After Marty left the diner, he drove home, showered the filth of the poker game from his skin, and made a cup of instant coffee. He drank the coffee and went downtown to the bank again. Or, rather, to the two banks. At one bank, where he had a checking account under the name Martin Granger, he deposited the five hundred dollars on which he was willing to pay taxes. In the other bank, where he had a safe deposit box under the name Henry Adams, he deposited a thousand dollars on which he did not intend to pay taxes. The remaining thirteen hundred dollars stayed in his money belt. A gambler had to have a roll, and he had to keep it with him all the time. Otherwise he missed too much worthwhile action for lack of funds.

Then he had gone home again, and to bed. He was exhausted—it had literally been days since he had had any sleep and he was ready to fall apart. He sprawled nude on the bed in his air-conditioned bedroom and slept like a hibernating bear.

He awoke at seven. He had a constitutional inability to sleep for more than seven hours at a stretch. Even after a several-day siege at a poker table, he still woke after seven hours. He showered again, dressed in a white short-sleeved shirt and a pair of twenty-dollar gabardine slacks, and went to the kitchen. He made himself two ham-and-swiss sandwiches and washed them down with two bottles of imported German beer. He got a pack of Luckies from the refrigerator—they stayed fresher there—and he smoked three of them. Then he left his house and got in the Olds.

He remembered the waitress, Betty, big boobs and swinging rear. He remembered her and he realized how much he needed a woman. It was always that way after a long game, more so when he won than when he lost. Poker established necessary tensions. You couldn't play when you were completely relaxed, because then the game didn't matter enough to you. The tensions didn't go away when the game was over. Instead, they transformed themselves into sexual tensions. These could be dispelled only by the possession of a woman's body. All other forms of therapy—tranquilizers, liquor, sleep—were futile.

Marty started the car, drove through the center of town to the border area. He drove across, parked the big Olds on one of the main streets. Otherwise, he knew, the kids would strip off the hubcaps, the radio, aerial, the side mirror. This was standard in Juarez, and on occasion, they jacked up cars and took the tires as well.

He parked, locked the car, left it. He stopped at a tavern for a bottle of Dos Equis, the dark Mexican beer that was almost as good as the German stuff he had at home, and that cost him only twelve cents a bottle. He finished the beer and walked over by the plaza.

The thing to do, he knew, was to head across the park to the whorehouse area. There were row upon row of cribs there, one-room shacks where the girls went around the world for a dollar and a half, but he was not interested in the cribs. There were other places, hazily disguised as night clubs and geared to con visiting nuns from Nebraska into thinking the clubs were just for dancing and drinking. In these places the girls were genuinely beautiful, and you paid them five dollars and made love to them on a clean bed. He would go home to Paso five dollars poorer and able, at last, to relax.

But he was in no hurry. A prostitute was better than a girl like Betty, because with a whore you knew exactly where you stood, you bought something and you paid for it and that was all. With a whore, you didn't have to worry about getting rid of her in the morning. With a whore it was just business, even if the Mex girls did put their hearts into it well enough to con you into thinking it was love. With Betty it would be a pain later on, and it was well worth a fast five bucks to avoid such pain.

But a prostitute, while better than Betty, was several shades removed from Nirvana. What Marty Granger wanted was a girl he could respect and lay at the same time.

Good luck finding one on the streets of Juarez. He was a gambler, but he was also a smart gambler. He did not draw to inside straights. Nor did he look for a respectable lay when he needed a piece so bad be could taste it.

He passed the brunette almost without seeing her. No, he saw her—but the image didn't really register until he was a few steps beyond her. Then he remembered the long black hair, the perfect legs that showed beneath the skirt, long legs crossed at the knee and delicately tanned. He remembered, too, that the brunette had been looking at something.

He turned around and saw that she was looking at porno-graphic photos. Now some men might have been able to go on walking, and unless such men were homosexuals they were men with whom Marty would have been unhappy to play poker. They would have been able to run a bluff through the entire Tenth Army.

So he stopped and said. "Well, hello. What have you got there?"

And she said, "I've got filthy pictures here. Have a seat and have a look, friend."

He had a seat and a look. He had a look first at the pictures, and he had a look second down the front of the girl's dress. He knew, instantly, that he was not going to find a prostitute. Any woman with this much poise was miles out of Betty's class. Any woman with this much poise would be about eighteen times as exciting as a Juarez Five-Dollar Businessman's Special.

"I like this one," she said, showing him a picture of a five-person orgy. "Ever do anything like this?"

"Never."

"Neither have I. I had a husband up until a day or two ago, and it was rare enough to do much of anything with him. Now I'm divorced. Are you married?"

"No."

"Ever been married?"

"Never."

"It's horrible. Never marry, friend."

He took out his Luckies and shook two from the pack. He lit both cigarettes and gave one to her.

"Looking at this picture is making me horny," she said. "Do you like straightforward and direct women?"

"Yes."

"Well," she said, "I want to get laid and I haven't had a man in awfully long. I'm being straightforward and direct as hell, friend. I'm horny as hell, too. I want to get laid. I don't even know your name but I want to get laid."

"It's Marty."

"Mine's Meg. Interested, Marty?

"I'm interested."

"Just look at these lovely pictures," she said, spreading out three or four of them on her lap. "I want to do it this way and this way and this way. I don't know about this one, though. Ever do it this way?"

"Yes," he said.

"Is it fun?"

"It's okay."

"Then this way, too. I've never been in Juarez before. Do you go to a hotel or just make love in the park like the natives?"

"I've got a house."

"Here?"

"In Paso," he said. "I've got a car and we can be there in five minutes."

"That sounds about right," she said. "I think I can hold out for five minutes. God, I'm horny. I'm a little bit drunk, too. Very drunk, actually. But I won't pass out on you or anything. I'll be fine."

"Will you hate yourself in the morning?"

"Only if you're lousy in bed. If you're good, I'll love myself in the morning. Let's go, Marty."

She got to her feet and he helped her shovel the filthy pictures back into her purse. She took his arm. He led her to the Olds, deciding that he liked this Meg, that she was all right. She was drunk, and she probably would be a little different when she was sober, but the direct and straightforward routine seemed honest enough.

She was going to be good in bed, he knew. Very good in bed. She was horny and hungry and ready to go, and he was hot from need and hot from the pictures and hot from her, and it would be a long night.

He grinned at her. "If I'm real good will you do more than love yourself in the morning?"

"I'll love you too," she replied with a sly smile.

"How?"

"The same way I did during the night."

"The *same* way," he said with a sigh of disappointment.

"Well," she explained, "by morning we may have to repeat ourselves and do it one way for the second time."

"Are you up to it?" he asked.

"I'm up to it as long as you're up to me," she said.

"I will be—close up to you—in five minutes."

They were at the side of his Olds now. He unlocked the door on the passenger side and held it open for her. She seated herself gracefully and he looked down her dress again. She had better breasts than Betty, he saw. Very fine breasts.

His hands itched with need to touch, to hold. He drew a breath, walking around the Olds and pitching his half-smoked cigarette into the gutter. She leaned across the seat to open the door for him and he had another look at her breasts. She was wearing a bra. It would be a pleasure to take it off.

He got into the car, rolled down his window, started the car. She leaned forward and switched off the ignition.

"First give me a kiss," she said.

He kissed her and her tongue leaped into his mouth. She drew close, thrusting her breasts against his chest, clutching at his hair with her fingers.

"Now give me a feel," she said.

He put his hand on her breast and cupped it, feeling the weight of it, the warmth of it, the softness of it.

"Now drive like hell," she said. "Drive like hell."

He increased the movements of his hand over her breasts and turned his body slightly toward her.

"No," she protested. "Drive the car like hell. You can drive me like hell later."

He slipped his hands from her breasts to the ignition and steering wheel.

The engine roared.

He shifted and then stepped on the gas.

The car lunged forward and Meg's body jerked. She steadied herself but her breasts kept moving. They jerked upward and then back, and then bounced.

Marty kept watching them and began to remove one hand from the steering wheel.

"The road!" she screamed. "Watch out!"

He heard the scraping sounds of wheels on gravel and felt the hard bounces as the car went onto the shoulder of the road.

Then his eyes were back on the road and he jerked the wheel quickly to the left.

The car shot back onto the road and then continued to roar straight ahead.

Marty's head was throbbing and his heart was pounding and his breath was heavy.

But was it from that near accident or from her, he wondered.

"Take it easy, Marty," she said, "If we're going to get ourselves killed, let's at least do it after we try those positions."

CHAPTER THREE

Lily was on her way across the border when the blue Olds roared past her. She looked up and saw the man at the wheel and the long-haired brunette at his side. Then the car was gone and she forgot them. She was across the border now, in Juarez, and it wasn't such a big deal after all. Just another town, full of Mexicans instead of Americans, and that was about it.

Still, she thought, almost anything was a hell of a distance better than the Paso hotel where she was staying. Cappy's Hotel, the home of every flying ant and palmetto bug in Texas. A humming fan and a squeaking dripping sink and tenants who never washed. A wiry and ugly gink who stared at her when he passed her in the hallway. They could take Cappy's Hotel, she decided, and they could shove it. It was cheap enough, and it would do until she could either connect with somebody or get her hands on some long bread. All she had for the time being was what remained of the two tens she'd gotten from the jerko who had driven her to El Paso. Two bucks had gone to Cappy, whoever he was, and three bucks and change had gone for food, and two bucks more had gone for a clean blouse. That left her with somewhere between twelve and thirteen dollars. Hardly enough to retire on. Hardly enough to feel particularly secure about.

Juarez. The first step was to find the right people, the kind of people she could swing with. These were the sort of people she had known in North Beach and she knew that she would find them again in Juarez. Border towns were attractive areas for that sort. They would avoid the American side and stay on the Mex side because things were cheaper and freer and easier there. You paid less for food and drink, and you bought marijuana with relative impunity, and if you were on the harder stuff it was easier and less expensive to make a connection with a pusher.

She was in Juarez, and she was cruising. She stopped at a corner to catch her breath, spat with annoyance when a pair of dirty-faced Mexican urchins tried to beg a few coins from her, then continued onward. Her feet led her along almost intuitively. Denver had had its own little hard core of the hip cognoscenti and S.F. had had many more, and Lily had known them well in both towns. It was easy to guess what street might hold a place where particular people would be congregating. It was easy to pass some bars without a second glance, easy to turn at the proper street and walk into the proper Mexican tavern. She did all this intuitively and it took her less than a half hour before she found precisely the place she had been looking for from the beginning.

A small frame building, painted years ago and drab now. A scattering of sawdust on the floor. Brown wood, varnished once, the varnish long worn away by time. A small bar with six stools. A Mex behind the bar, old and white-haired. Four or five tables, two of them round, the rest square. Five kids in their twenties at one of the round tables, with a bottle of tequila in the middle of the table. Two Mexicans and one bearded American wearing an army field jacket at the bar. Two gaunt girls at one of the square tables. A couple—an old man with a young wife—at another square table. No one else in the place.

Lily's eyes took all this in quickly. She walked directly to the big round table. There was a chair open between a flat-chested redhead and a boy with a scraggly brown beard. She sat at the chair, took the redhead's empty glass and poured an ounce or so of tequila into it. She threw the firewater straight down and didn't choke on it.

Someone said, "Who, baby?"

"Lily Daniels. Out of Denver by North Beach. No money and no friends. This seat wasn't taken, was it, man?"

"It is now. Stay as cool as you are, baby."

She smiled at a clean-shaven man with horn-rimmed glasses. He pushed the bottle back at her. "Have some more juice, Lily girl. We're way out in front of you."

She poured another short shot and tossed it off. "Solid," she said. "Solid."

"You in town long?"

"Just today. I thumbed from Big D to Paso, got in a little past noon. What's happening?"

The flat-chested redhead laughed. The scraggly brown beard said, "I been around S.F. You know a cat name of Randy Kapper?"

"Tall thin cat," she said. "A cocaine habit."

"When I knew him he sniffed a little. He hooked now?"

"Through the bag and back again."

"That's a bitch," the scraggly beard said. "He was a nice cat, when I knew him. He was padding out with Renee, I don't know her last name, a big blonde with a fat can. Then she turned around to make a lesbo scene and Randy was all hung up. That's a bitch, though, him on a coke needle. You never know."

They played who-do-you-know for fifteen minutes. They tossed mutual acquaintances back and forth and managed to get introductions across without being formal about it. The scraggly brown beard was Artie, the horn-rimmed glasses was Paul, the flat-chested redhead was Cassie. There was another girl with short dark hair named Didi and a blinking, red-eyed boy named Benno. Lily had more tequila.

"You dig Mary Juanita, Lily?"

"I've been there. I can take it or put it down."

"Why's that?"

"I don't smoke regular cigarettes," she said, "So it's kind of hard for me to groove on pot. My throat gets like sandpaper."

More talk and more tequila. The bearded American left the bar and walked out into the night. The two Mexicans got into an argument. One of them took out a knife, pressed a button. A blade shot forward. The other Mexican picked up a beer bottle by the base and snapped the neck off deftly on the bartop. The bartender, white-haired and sad-eyed, spoke rapid Spanish to both of them. The knife was folded and returned to a pocket, the broken bottle replaced on the top of the bar.

"I thought we'd see action," Paul said lazily. "No action any-more. You got any bread, Lily?"

"None." They didn't have to know about her twelve dollars. She was hanging onto it for the time being. Let them pay for the tequila, if they wanted to. Not her, thank you.

"No bread? How you plan on eating?"

"I don't know."

Artie said, "Maybe Cassie can get you a gig. Cassie's got a good job, Lily-O."

Cassie was blushing, her face as red as her hair.

"Cassie's in show biz," Artie went on, his lips twitching in the beginning of a smile. "She has this gig at a night club, like. A club called Delia's Place. You could say she's the floorshow."

Cassie shifted uncomfortably in her chair. Lily poured another shot of tequila, the last in the bottle. She threw it down and drew a breath. She wondered what the redhead was squirming about.

"Maybe Cassie can get a job for you," Artie pressed on. "Where she works, like."

"I don't dance," Lily said.

Benno broke up over that one. "She don't dance," he said. "Son of a bitch, she don't dance!"

"I said something funny?"

"Funny," Artie said. "Cassie don't dance either. Tell her about your gig, Cassie Kid. Lily might wig over it."

Cassie said, "Delia's Place is a cathouse, like. There's a floor-show, you know, and then you go with the customers. That's all. I'm not in show business. It's Artie's idea of a joke. He has this sense of humor."

Artie started laughing again.

"Is the pay good?"

"She don't care about the money," Benno said, breaking up all over again. "She does it cause she digs the work. The money's just extra."

Cassie told him to shut up. "The money could be better or worse," she told Lily. "A girl makes ten times as much hustling in the States, because here there's a million Mexican whores and they damn near give it away. But it still isn't bad. I get about thirty a day and it's just a few hours and they don't care if you come on a little bit stoned as long as it doesn't slow you down. The guy who runs the place is an American, he used to live in New York."

Lily was beginning to feel the tequila. Her head was lighter than usual and all her muscles felt loose and relaxed. She reached for the bottle to pour another shot, then remembered it was empty and let her hand drop.

Cassie's job didn't sound too bad. A week ago she wouldn't have thought about it for a minute, but that was before the red-neck in the Dallas hotel and, more significantly, before the driver in the air-conditioned Buick. It wasn't hard to ball with a stranger. All you did was squirm around and let him have his kicks. You didn't have to feel it yourself. He was just using your body, and that didn't matter much.

"It doesn't sound too bad," Lily said.

"You want to meet Ringo? He's the guy who runs the place."

"I'll meet him."

"I don't know if he wants anybody," Cassie said. "But we can see, and you can see if you dig it. Later, everybody."

Lily stood up. Now, on her feet, she really felt the drinks. Her head was swimming. She followed the flat-chested redhead out of the bar and walked with her down the street.

Meg was slowly scratching herself. She lay flat on her back with no pillow beneath her head and scratched herself lazily, liking the way it felt. Not that it really needed scratching, now. It had been scratched expertly by an expert, and it had been scratched more than once.

Meg glanced at the expert. His eyes were closed and he was smoking a cigarette.

She said, "Marty."

"Mmmm?"

"That was good, Marty."

"I know. I needed it."

"So did I. Cigarette?"

He lit one and handed it to her. She took a drag and savored the smoke in her lungs. A cigarette tasted much better afterward. Everything was better.

"One thing I don't understand, Marty. You're a single guy. Why the hell do you have a house?"

"Don't you like the house?"

"Sure, but—"

"I could have an apartment," he said. "A decent apartment would cost me a hundred and a quarter a month. I pay eighty a month on the house and I have three times as much room and five times as much privacy and no landlord. So why pay rent?"

"And when the mortgage is paid you'll own the house."

"It's a twenty-year mortgage," he said. "And a post-war house. I don't figure it'll be standing in twenty years."

"You own a house and you still drive a six-year old car. Why?"

"Don't you *like* the car?"

"Well, sure, but—"

"It runs like a clock," he said. "It gets an oil change every five hundred miles and it goes to the garage once a month for a check-up. Every piece of iron on that car is better than when it left Detroit six years ago. I couldn't buy that good a car no matter what I paid. Why get a new car?"

She nodded thoughtfully. Borden had driven a Chrysler Imperial, and he had traded once a year, whenever the new model came out. He was a terrible driver and something was always wrong with whatever car they had owned at the time.

"Could you afford a new car?"

He thought a moment. "I could afford a Rolls Royce," he said finally. "But I don't need one. I could afford to pay cash for a Rolls Royce. I like the Olds, though."

"You have a lot of money?"

"I have enough."

"Are you in the rackets?"

"Would I tell you, Meg?"

"You might."

He put out his cigarette. "I was in the rackets once, on the coast. I left with no hard feelings. I was just an errand boy and I didn't like the work."

"What do you do now?"

"I gamble and win. I play poker, mainly. Sometimes dice, but I don't like dice. I don't like anything where you're playing against mathematics instead of against other people. Poker you play against people, and if you're good you win."

"And you're good."

"Otherwise I'd lose."

She digested this. Borden had liked the roulette wheel at Vegas, and had lost a great deal of money. He played poker once a week with business friends. He invariably lost, and cursed his luck daily.

"Do you have a job Marty?"

"No. I don't need one."

"Do you play cards every day?"

He laughed. "No. Maybe once a week. Sometimes not even that often. When some good action comes along, I play. That's all."

"And the rest of the time?"

"I just take things easy."

"By yourself?"

He looked over at her lying beside him. "Not always."

She finished her cigarette and gave it to him to put out. He took a last drag, butted the cigarette in the ashtray. "I would think there would be more poker games in a bigger city," she said. "Like New York or Chicago or Los Angeles."

"There are."

"Why do you stay in El Paso, then?"

"I get enough action to keep me going. And this way I don't break laws. You can get arrested in the States, playing in a heavy game. If the fix isn't in well enough, the cops can pick you up and cart you off to jail. I don't have a record and I want to keep it that way."

"The games are across the border?"

"That's right. In Juarez. There's probably a Mexican law against gambling but it's never enforced. They barely enforce the laws against murder in Mexico. They don't have time to worry about a quiet poker game." He stopped, thought for a moment. "There are some crooked games," he went on, "where suckers get taken with marked cards, stuff like that. Those games get broken up now and then because it can hurt the tourist trade. But I'm not interested in crooked games. They're no kick."

Meg said, "I like you."

"Good."

"You're good for me." she went on. "You know what I want, Marty? I want to let go, I mean of everything, just let go and let the world spin out on its string all over the place. I want excitement. I want to do everything and see everything."

"You're in the right place."

"El Paso, you mean?"

"I mean Juarez."

"It's exciting?"

"Whatever you want, it's here. Sex, drugs, gambling, liquor, everything. It's all here."

"Do you take advantage of it?"

"Not much. I'm not a tourist. I just live here."

"We could take advantage of it together," she said. "We could go wild, Marty. We could let the whole world spin its string out for us. Would you like that?"

"I might."

"Is Juarez still open? Could we do anything tonight?"

"It's open until dawn."

"Can we go?"

"Tomorrow."

"Not tonight?"

"Not tonight, Meg. I want you again. And then I want to go to sleep."

She didn't say anything. He rolled over onto his side, slowly, and she turned to face him. His hand reached for her, touched her shoulders, moved very slowly to her breast. She had thought she was through for the night but the minute he touched her breast she realized she had been mistaken. His hands sent her reeling again.

"Marty—"

"Shut up," he said. "Don't talk."

His hand was busy with her breast. He fondled it, patted it. He took a nipple between two fingers and began to caress the taut flesh until she wanted to shriek. His other hand was on her thigh now, moving higher.

She could not remain still. Her own hands reached for him, found him. She touched him and his eyes blazed with need for her. His hand moved from her thigh, higher, and found her. His fingers played with her, teasing her, and she grew warm for him. She was trembling inside.

She rolled over, onto her back, and he moved above her. He had his hands on her breasts now and he worked them. She thought she was going to be torn apart, to die. She gripped him pulling him closer.

He touched her. Then, fiercely, he drove into her, and she surrounded him. His body drove at her, again and again and again, and the excitement was here, the passion was here—

At the moment of fulfillment—towering, shrieking, frighteningly powerful fulfillment—her nails clawed his back and buttocks and his teeth bit into her shoulder. She screamed, once. The sound that tore from her lips was not remotely human.

Then he was saying, "Now go to sleep. Tomorrow we'll find some excitement, if you want."

She would have answered him but she was too empty to move, to speak, even to think. She closed her eyes and slept.

Ringo was around forty-five, with a pot belly and bandy legs. He had long glossy black hair that he combed carefully over a bald spot on the top of his head. He looked from Cassie to Lily, then back to Cassie, then at Lily once more. His eyes travelled over her body. He looked at her breasts and at her hips.

"I don't know," he said.

"She's good-looking," Cassie said. "Man, you know that much, don't you?"

"Maybe."

He took a cigar from his pocket, unwrapped it, bit off the end, spat, and lit the cigar. To Lily he said, "Peel. I want to see what you look like without clothes on."

She didn't argue. She took off the blouse and the khakis. She was wearing no bra, because the Texan in Dallas had ruined the only one she owned. She wasn't wearing underwear, either. Her panties had been dirty, and she hadn't had a chance to rinse them out.

"The boobs are real and you're blonde all over," he said. "That's a help, anyway. Nice boobs."

He was not looking at her the way men usually did. His eyes were cool and impersonal. He was a businessman studying a commodity, trying to decide whether it was worth buying, whether he could make a decent profit on it. "Get dressed," he said at length, and she put her clothes back on.

"Well?" Cassie looked at Ringo. "She hired, man?"

"I don't know." He chewed the cigar. "You hustle any, kid?"

"I been laid, if that's what you mean."

"So have I," Ringo said. "But I'd make a lousy whore. You do any hustling?"

"A little."

"I don't mean giving it away. I mean for money?"

"A little."

"You can't play prude here." Ringo said. "Some broads want to hustle but won't turn anything but straight tricks. That's fine if you're in the States, maybe. These Mex broads'll do anything in the world. You draw the line, you can't work here."

"I don't draw the line."

"Some guy'll want you to talk to 'em in French. You know how to speak French?"

She remembered the second act with the man in the Dallas hotel room. She told Ringo that she could speak French.

"And Greek?"

"And Greek."

"Well, that's something. Still, I don't know. This isn't just a cathouse operation I got here. This is like a club, you understand. We have floorshows. We get an expensive clientele, serve the best food and the best liquor and give 'em entertainment you can't find on Broadway. They can find whores for five bucks and get good ones, but this is a package deal and that's what brings them around. The show is full now. I don't see where you'd fit."

For a moment no one said anything. Lily waited for something to happen. Now, strangely, it seemed important for her to get the job. She wanted it badly.

"Ringo," Cassie said, "I got an idea."

"I'm listening."

"Lily an' I could do an act. A gay act."

"We've had that and it's nothing new."

"You've had it with Mex chicks. Think about it with us. A redhead and a blonde on the stage. Picture it, Ringo. It's twice as hot for a tourist to see a redhead and a blonde up there, both Americans. Twice as hot."

Ringo looked thoughtful. "It might go."

"It'll go, Ringo. You know it'll go."

Ringo chewed the cigar. "You start tomorrow," he told Lily. "You get here ten in the evening, do your number with Cassie here, then put out for whoever wants a piece of you. You get ten for the special and two bucks every time you turn a trick. Okay?"

She looked at Cassie, who was nodding her head. "Okay," she said. "I'll see you."

Outside she said, "I don't know, Cassie. This is a lesbo number he's talking about. Right?"

"Right."

"Well, I don't know."

The redhead looked at her. "You never made it with a chick?"

"No."

"It's a groove," Cassie said. "It's better that way. Something different."

"Are you a dyke?"

"I work both ways, Lily. You shocked?"

"I don't shock easy."

"I didn't think so. Listen, I work four or five hours a night doing it with men, balling with 'em. It's like a drag after a while. You need a change of pace now and then. You know Didi, she was at the bar there?"

"I remember her."

"I was making it with Didi for a while. Then she decided to straighten out. She flipped over Paul and she's shacking with him now, spending all her time at his pad."

"And I'm supposed to take her place? Is that the general idea, Cassie?"

Cassie shrugged, "You can try it on and find out if it fits or not. That's all."

Lily thought about it. Hell, she decided, everybody had an angle. Cassie was tickled magenta to put her up for a good-pay job, but Cassie wanted a payoff for her part in the game. She smiled to herself, thinking how neatly the redhead had set it up. Even if she didn't want to go along with it, even if she stayed away from Cassie except for working hours, she still would make love to the girl once a night. On stage.

And who knew—it could even be fun. Balling was balling, and it shouldn't make a hell of a difference whether you were balling with a man or a woman. The equipment was different, maybe, but that was about it. If it was a kick to make it with Cassie, she'd enjoy herself. If it was a drag, she would tolerate it.

"I suppose I could try," she said.

"Solid."

"But aren't you working tonight?"

"I'm taking a night off." They were walking along a poorly lighted street, walking in the middle of the street because there was no sidewalk. Cassie let her arm go around Lily. Lily didn't flinch.

"A night off," Cassie said. "For the rehearsal."

"The rehearsal?"

"That's the bit. We have to make it for an audience tomorrow night. So we spend tonight getting our lines straight. You never balled a chick before, Lily. Lots of things I've got to teach you, like."

"Yeah, I dig."

"I do too."

"The first lesson then."

"Oh, maybe the second and the third ones too. I'm offering a special tonight."

"A special price or a special lesson?"

"Both," Cassie smiled.

"All right."

"I knew you were the night school type."

"You got a pad?"

"A few blocks. We're on our way right now."

"What kind of a pad?"

"A room in a dumpy hotel. They don't ask questions there. It's practically a whorehouse itself. A batch of Mex girls sit in the bar downstairs and guys pick 'em up and take 'em to their rooms."

"Yeah. I'm hip to that scene."

"Sometimes you can go down there and pick up a trick yourself."

"After work?"

"Yeah. Bring in a little extra bread that way. You can't depend on it but you can take your pick—and you don't have to share the bread with anyone."

Lily nodded in understanding.

"Last week I picked up a crazy trick. Taught me something new. I tried it at Ringo's and it went over big. The customers were so happy that Ringo gave me a bonus."

Lily didn't reply.

"Maybe we could try it tonight, eh, Lily baby?"

Lily shrugged her shoulders.

"I've always wondered whether two chicks could do that together," Cassie said.

Her arm tightened about Lily's shoulder.

At the corner they turned, and Lily could see lights up ahead. Cassie's hand dropped from shoulder to breast.

"You got about the nicest boobs I ever saw." Cassie was whispering hoarsely. "I was hot as hell when you peeled for Ringo. I wanted to jump you then and there."

Now Cassie's fingers were pinching a nipple. Lily smiled to herself. It didn't make any difference, she thought. The hand could have been Cassie's or a man's—it made no difference at all.

It's what the hand was doing to her, that was important, she thought. And *what* it was doing to her. The fingers on her nipple, the warmth of the rest of the hand between her breasts, spreading the soft flesh.

Cassie ran her hand back and forth between the two mounds of flesh and the softness molded itself, around her hand.

Then her fingers slipped down and under and gently lifted.

"Nice, nice, nice," Cassie repeated. "You're so nice there. Wait till we get to my pad and I'll really show you some scenes with those boobs of yours."

Her hand was darting in and out and around now.

"Just wait," Cassie was saying now, her lips close to Lily's ear. "Just wait. I'm going to show you everything, Lily. Everything there is to know. Baby, you'll dig it. I know you will."

"Maybe."

"And you're blonde all the way, aren't you? Hell, don't answer, baby. Like I saw it myself."

"Yeah."

"Well, I'm a redhead all the way. You like?"

"Sure, Cassie."

Cassie stopped, turned Lily around. "Come on," she said. "I'm like so crazy for it I can't stand it. Give me a kiss, Lily."

"Here in the street?"

"Nobody's looking."

"Well, sure."

Lily reached out her arms, let the redheaded girl come close. Their mouths came together and Lily found out what it was like to kiss a girl. It was different. Cassie's mouth was softer than any man's mouth had been, and Cassie's body was different in her arms. When Cassie's little pink tongue stole between Lily's lips, Lily was surprised to find herself responding to the embrace.

"You feel it, don't you?"

"I feel it."

"Well, you'll feel it even more back at my pad," Cassie whispered into her ear. "You'll feel it there and someplace else. You'll feel it, and that feeling will mount and grow and spread inside you. You'll feel all those feelings meet and join. You'll feel it lift you up into space and speed through you until you crash through the heat barrier."

"I feel it now," Lily whispered.

"And you like it, right?"

"So far I like it."

"Oh, Lily. Oh, baby. There's a lot more, Lily, and you'll like it, baby, you'll love it. You'll scream and you'll beg for more, you'll just love it. That's where it's at, baby."

And they hurried to the hotel.

CHAPTER FOUR

Weaver finished the horror comic and hurled it across the room. It was the third time he had read that particular comic book and on this final reading it had not held his interest at all. He took a long shuddering breath and pressed his face down into his pillow.

He could not sleep. It was late, past three in the morning, and he had been trying to fall asleep since well before midnight. He would close his eyes and lie in darkness, listening only to the monotonous whine of the overhead fan, and he would wait for sleep to come to him. This it refused to do. Time after time he got up, switched on the light, crawled back into his clothes. Sometimes he would re-read one of the horror comics. Other times he would scuttle down the hall to the bathroom to void his bladder. Finally he would try again to sleep, and would fail again.

He sat up now, walked to the stack of comics, picked one up. On the cover a gorilla held a woman high overhead, one hand on her bare thigh and the other wrapped around her neck. The gorilla was standing on the edge of a chasm and he was preparing to heave the woman onto the jagged rocks below. Weaver studied the picture for a moment. He sighed, and dropped the book back onto the stack.

The hotel room was suffocating him. He had to get out, had to go somewhere and do something before he went out of his mind. He needed something. He was not sure what he needed, did not even want to think about what it might be that his nervous system demanded. But whatever it was, he needed it.

He stood before the mirror over the washbowl, wetted his hair and combed it. He left the hotel room, walked to a flight of stairs, descended them quickly. Some of the stairs creaked when he stepped on them. The cracking stairs had an eerie sound and he was glad to reach the first floor.

There was a very old man behind the desk. He looked up at Weaver, caught the key that Weaver tossed to him. He looked away without speaking and Weaver went out of the door onto the street. At an all-night cafeteria he had an order of french toast and sausages with a cup of coffee. The toast was good but the sausages were greasy and he had to leave most of them on his plate. He had another cup of coffee. He put three teaspoons of sugar into each cup and filled it to the brim with cream.

After he left the cafeteria, the two cups of coffee sloshing inside him, he was not any sleepier. El Paso was a daylight town, quiet at night, and he walked the streets alone without seeing a single person. The main street of the downtown section was dark and quiet. Only a few stores left their neon signs on at night; fewer had their windows illuminated. Weaver walked and walked and saw no one.

He was used to the night, and to silent walks down silent streets. In Tulsa, before the killing, before the little girl who had been so foolish as to ask him the time, he had been essentially a creature of the night. A quiet man. A man who worked eight hours a day, five days a week, as a stockroom clerk in a Lincoln Drive department store. A man who earned forty-five dollars a week, week after week. Each summer they gave him two weeks off, with full pay, and he spent his vacations in Tulsa, going to movies, reading comic books, taking long walks.

He had no friends in Tulsa. He spoke to no one at work and no one spoke to him. He was ugly, and he was not very bright, and he had no personality as far as anyone knew. He avoided people, and they were delighted to be avoided by him.

At night, he walked. The night was as exciting as the day was drab, because the night was dark and a man could walk without being seen, could walk through dark streets like a ghost across the Scottish moors. A man like Weaver could look through windows as women took off their clothes. If he was lucky, very lucky, he could look through windows while married men made love to their wives. Weaver had been a nobody in Tulsa, a man who had never done a thing. He had never made love to a woman, had never so much as kissed a woman. He was an orphan, with no family. A nobody.

Now, walking through El Paso by night, he was at least a some-body for once. He knew this, and in a weird way the knowledge was comforting. He had Done Something. The Something was a horrible thing, but he had done it, and they had put his pic-ture in the newspapers and had broadcast his name over the radio. They called him Dracula, and they called him the Cannibal Killer, but now, for the first time, they knew who he was.

And this made him feel good, somehow. It was better to be loathed as a fiend than to be thoroughly ignored, better to be hated than not to be known at all. One act of horror had given direction to his life, had elevated him from *no*body to *some*body.

He went on walking. The sky was streaked with false dawn. He walked surely now, his stride powerful, his arms swinging easily at his side. He was the Angel of Death, he thought. His life had a mission, a strange and terrifying sense of purpose.

He thought now of that little girl in Tulsa. He realized now that he had made several significant errors in his thinking. Before, that girl had seemed to have been a dreadful mistake, an end. But she was not an end at all. She was a beginning. She was the first person he had killed.

She would not be the last.

And, with this re-evaluation of the girl's role, he came also to a new understanding of his procedure from that point on. Capture was inevitable, he knew. Sooner or later he would be caught by the police, caught and beaten and killed. But until then it was not enough merely to go on living, merely to hide like a scared rabbit and wait for the inevitable closing of the net around him.

He had to be positive in his behavior. He had to go on killing, had to seek out other girls, had to do to them as he had done to the thirteen-year-old girl in Tulsa. Fresh killings would not hurt him. The police could not beat him any more brutally for additional corpses. And death in the electric chair, when it came, would be just as painful and just as final no matter how many girls died at his hands.

False dawn gave way to real dawn. Weaver went to another cafeteria and had another breakfast, this time a plate of scrambled eggs and an order of toast and jelly. He left the cafeteria and walked again, finally finding a store where they sold razors. He bought an old-fashioned straight razor. The salesman asked him if he wanted a leather strop as well. He told the man he already owned one.

He walked back to the hotel. He put the razor away in a dresser drawer under some clothing. It was a sharp razor, and he liked it already. Soon, he thought, there would be blood upon the blade.

The stack of horror comics was where he had left it. He picked up each comic, tore it in half, and dropped it into the wastebasket beneath the washbowl. He did not need the comic books anymore. He did not need to live his life through pictures and balloon dialogue. He would live an active life now.

He went to bed and slept well.

❋

Marty woke up at ten. He and Meg had called it a night around three, and as usual he could not sleep more than seven hours at a stretch. He got out of bed and walked to the bathroom, deciding that he must have a clock in his head, the way he never slept more. It was strange, because the sense of timing only worked when he was unconscious. During the day he never knew what time it was. When playing cards he lost all track, never knew whether he'd been playing for three hours or nine hours. But when he slept, somehow he always knew.

Meg was sleeping soundly. He took hold of her shoulder, shook her gently. Her eyes remained closed.

He showered and shaved. He came back and she was still sound asleep. He took a pencil and a scrap of paper and wrote her a note, telling her that she could fix herself breakfast, that he would be back soon. He got dressed and went outside to the garage, got into the Olds and drove away.

The sun was bright, the sky clear of clouds. Marty decided that it would be a good day to pass up seeing Betty, the bouncy waitress. He found another diner where he'd been a few times before. He sat at the counter, had ham and fried eggs sunny side up and three cups of coffee. In this diner there was no waitress, just a counterman with tattoos on both arms and a surly expression on his face. The counterman didn't say two words to Marty in the course of the meal. Marty decided that this was fine, and much better than Betty and her big tits. He decided to eat breakfast there regularly. The food was just as good, and they let you eat it in peace.

He smoked three Luckies, one with each cup of coffee. He left the lunch counter and drove the blue Olds to a cigar store a half mile away. The clerk looked up at him when he entered and smiled a hello. Marty waited while the clerk finished selling a pack of pipe tobacco to a man in a blue cord suit. When the man had left, Marty walked closer to the counter.

He said, "What's the word?"

The clerk scratched his bald head. "A feller was around last night," he said. "Looking for a gin rummy game. You play gin rummy, don't you?"

"When I can't help it."

"Well, he was looking for a game. He drove up in a fishtail Cadillac with Florida plates on her."

"What stakes does he play?"

"He said something about a dollar a point. Hollywood, spades double. I think that's the way he said it. I don't know gin rummy so I can't be sure, but that sounds about right. It mean anything?"

"It means an expensive game," Marty said. "A stupid game. You get a heavy hand and you fall on a lot of money. The cards do all the work. All you need is a card memory and a head for odds and the cards do the rest."

The clerk didn't say anything. Marty took out a cigarette, lit it. He said, "Maybe the guy's a card mechanic. Maybe he's hustling, looking for a mark."

"You mean a cheater?"

"Yeah."

"It don't appear so," the clerk said. "He came in here an' left a string of horse bets. Left two hundred dollars, with me, maybe a bit more."

"What did he play?"

"Long shots, mostly. Played 'em on the nose."

"Then he's not a crook," Marty said. "He's too stupid to be a crook. He's got too much money and he's looking for ways to lose it. A Miami Beach boyo heading across the country in his Cad and looking for action on the way. I don't want to play him."

"Why not?"

"He could get lucky and beat me. Gin is mostly luck, especially the rules he plays by. I don't like the game enough to play. I'll pass it up."

"Suit yourself," the clerk said. "You want any action?"

Marty took a five dollar bill from his wallet, passed it to the clerk. "Three and five in the double," he said. "That's all."

He left the cigar store. Marty wasn't a horse player. It didn't make sense to him. The books took a twenty percent cut and what was left wasn't worth it. But he liked to bet the daily double. All it cost him was five dollars, and when it ever came in it was like winning a lottery. The payoff was big enough to make it worthwhile.

He drove back to his house, slowly. He stopped on the way at a gas station and filled the tank with hi-test. He had the Mex kid check the oil and water and put air in the tires. He tipped the kid a dollar and headed home again.

Meg, he thought. That was a broad, that was the right kind of broad. Eyes open, brain working right. And good in bed, so good, giving as good as she got, meeting him halfway, needing him just as he needed her. Meg was fine. He was glad he had picked her up.

In front of him, a traffic light turned red. He double-clutched the car, down-shifted to second, eased the brake on. While he waited for the light to turn green again he thought some more about Meg. She said she wanted excitement. She wanted to let go of everything, that was the way she put it.

Well, fine. He could use a little of the same, a little letting go of everything. About a week, say. A week or so of dissipation, a week of hard hot lust and hard drinking and hard living, a week of hell on wheels. You could get all tied up, just living the same life every day. You could be building a box around yourself without realizing it, and all at once you were in the box and somebody was puttying up the air holes and pretty soon you couldn't breathe anymore. When that started to happen you had to kick like hell until the box fell apart.

Excitement—that was her word, that was what she wanted. He had told her that Juarez was a good place for it, which was true enough. It was a perfect place. There were a hundred different kinds of sex, a dozen places to gamble, a million ways to get high. The cops let you alone. You got high and got drunk and got picked and got laid, and when you were done you crawled across the border and everything was sane again. That was the way to do it. When the light changed he dropped into first, let out the clutch, shot across the intersection. He drove straight home and left the car outside, at the curb. Then he walked to the front door and unlocked it with his key.

He hoped Meg was up. He wanted to talk with her.

That morning, Lily let Cassie pay for breakfast. They ate in Juarez at a bar that served tacos and chili. Lily ate a big plate of chili and a pair of chicken tacos and drank a bottle of orange soda. Cassie picked up the tab. She still didn't know about Lily's twelve dollars, and Lily saw no reason to clue her in. The less money she spent, the more she would wind up with. That much was elementary.

"Look," she said to Cassie, "I gotta get back to Paso. I left some stuff in the hotel. I want to get it."

"I'll come along."

"No."

"Why not? You sick of me, baby? I thought you had a good time last night."

"It was okay."

"Just okay?"

Lily looked at the redhead. "I got kicks," she said. "I dug what we were doing."

"I thought you did."

"But I have eyes to be alone." She thought for a moment, closing her eyes to concentrate. "I'm an introvert type," she went on. "I have to be alone some of the time or I get bugged. It's nothing against you, it's the way I swing, the way I move. I can't be around people too long or it gets to me and I flip a little."

"I'm hip. I know what you mean."

"So later," Lily said. "I'll go back to my crib for my stuff, then maybe catch a flick in Paso. I could dig sitting alone in an air-conditioned movie for a few hours."

"You got bread for a movie?"

"Some guy'll buy my way in. Some horny cat who wants a chick to sit next to him for a while. Once I'm inside I'll tell an usher he's bothering me and that'll get rid of him."

"You ever do that, Lily?"

"Once or twice."

"It sounds like a drag. Suppose the guy gives you a hard time?"

"They get the hint."

Cassie frowned. "He could wait outside," she said. "Follow you, maybe beat you up. It's not worth it."

The upshot of it was that Cassie pressed a five dollar bill into her palm, calling it a loan until Lily got her first pay for working at Delia's Place. It wasn't a loan, Lily knew. It was a present, and that was fine with her. She left Cassie at the Mex place and went back across the border to El Paso.

The five, added to her twelve, gave her seventeen. She put the five with the rest of the dough and started walking toward Cappy's, the hotel where she had been staying. There was nothing there that she needed, just a dirty old blouse she was planning to throw away. But she wanted to stay away from Cassie for the time being. The flat-chested redhead had a way of getting on her nerves over a period of time.

The night had been enjoyable enough. The novelty effect, first of all, was valuable. She had never before made it with another chick, partly because no dyke ever put the make on that strongly, partly because she had never thought of herself as a girl who could enjoy lesbian relations. But now that she'd been more or less forced into it, it wasn't bad at all.

To begin with, the whole sensation aspect was nothing new. It didn't make a hell of a big difference whether you had a cat or a chick going down on you—the same actions went on, and you felt the same way. Guys had gone down on her often enough in the past. Frank had almost always done so before they made love, and she had always enjoyed it. She enjoyed it even more with Cassie. Cassie was better at it, knew what she was doing. It was a kick.

The other side of the coin took some getting used to. Being caressed was one thing, while caressing was another. She never really managed to put her heart into that part, but she did what she was supposed to, conquering her initial revulsion and accepting it as part of the game. Evidently, she did it well enough. Cassie couldn't get too much of her; the dumb little redhead was half in love already, for Christ's sake.

Lily found Cappy's, went upstairs to her room. She took a bath in the bathroom down the hall, because there hadn't been a bathroom at the Mex place and she felt grimy all over. That was going to be one hunk of trouble about the job, she thought. Sex always made her feel scummy. And now she was going to take on a batch of men every night, plus the little show-biz routine with Cassie. She could hardly wash up between lays.

Hell, she thought. She could get used to it. And, if it got rough, she could always get a little edge on with tequila. The stuff half-burned your throat out, but it got to you in a hurry and gave you one hell of a buzz. And it was cheap as dishwater even if you had to pay for it all on your own, and cheaper still when someone else was picking up the check.

She lay back in the tub, letting the warm water hug her small pink body. She worked soap into her breasts, rubbing her own nipples and recalling the way Cassie's tongue had glided over her flesh, how Cassie's lips had closed around the nipples and pulled at them. She wondered idly how many men she would wind up taking on in the course of the evening. Cassie had said she earned around thirty or thirty-five bucks a night, and they were getting ten bucks each for the act on stage and two bucks a trick afterward. That meant she would make twenty to twenty-five from tricks and she'd be taking on ten to twelve men, maybe more on a good night.

That wasn't so bad. She'd been lined-up on once, back in Denver; it was the initiation for a clique at Western High and she had become a member. Six guys took her in turn and she had managed to live through it with no trouble, had even gotten her kicks out of the deal. A dozen guys was only double the six she'd been had by that night, and now it would be even easier, because she knew how to stay cool during sex, how to go through the motions without feeling a thing. She could let her body do all the work while her mind stayed neatly detached.

She finished her bath, dried off with a towel, went back to her room and put clothes on. She left the hotel without bothering to return the key. If Cassie turned out to be too much of a drag, she would just go on paying her two skins a night to live in El Paso. If Cassie was all right, she'd stay with the redhead at the hotel in Juarez. It would be cheaper, and it might be fun to have Cassie around.

At a cheap women's wear shop she picked up a pair of panties, a plaid skirt, and a fresh white blouse. She carried the bag with her when she went into a movie house on Coronado Avenue.

She walked directly to the ladies' room, where she changed her clothes, returning her dirty slacks and blouse to the paper bag. She stuffed the bag in a wastebasket and went downstairs to find a seat.

The movie was about a crowd of juvenile delinquents in Los Angeles. She kept breaking up all the way through it. Either the movie had its head up its tail or they did things a hell of a lot differently in L.A. She could tell them plenty.

Meg was happy. She had a cigarette between her lips and she drew on it now, taking in a lot of smoke. She relaxed in her seat in the front of the blue Olds and looked at Marty. He was driving, his hands on the wheel, his eyes straight ahead. He drove as he made love, letting nothing interfere with the attention he devoted to the subject at hand. She guessed that he played poker with the same single-minded dedication. If so, she could understand why he won. He was a perfect lover and a perfect driver, and he was probably a perfect card-player as well.

He had come in the door that morning just as she was finishing breakfast. She had awakened with a hangover, and breakfast had been in the form of an orange blossom, a glass of orange juice spiked with gin. He'd had the gin in a liquor cabinet in the living room and it had been no trouble finding it. The gin was Beefeater. There was also a fifth of Dewar's, a fifth of Jack Daniel's, a fifth of Old Overholt, and a quart of Smirnoff. They were, respectively, the best Scotch on the market, the best bourbon, the best rye, and the best vodka. She was beginning to understand something about Marty Granger. He did not bother with things that were second-rate. He liked the best.

She was flattered. He liked her, and this flattered her.

When he came home that morning he stood for a moment, looking at her, liking what he saw.

Then he said, "Let's go back to bed. I want you."

They went back to bed. He made the earth go around for her once again, made the top of her head come off. He kissed life into her big breasts and then he moved her thighs, plunging into her warmth and thrilling her to the depths of her being.

"We're going to the Casino Lupo," he told her now. "It's a gambling house on the outskirts of Juarez, a little ways south of the city. They've got roulette and baccarat and craps and chuckaluck. You ever gamble?"

"No."

"I'll give you two hundred to play with," he said. "You can see how you do. You ought to stick to the roulette wheel. Craps gives you a better percentage but you have to know the game. The rest is a way to toss money away, that's all. Baccarat, chuckaluck—the house gets too big an advantage. But you can move around if you want. We're not going there to win money. We're going so you can get a taste of gambling."

"What will you be doing?"

"They have a poker table," he said. "The house dealer stays out of the game. The house gets two bucks a pot. The game is stud, dollar ante, three dollar limit."

"Is that a lot?"

"It depends on what you're used to. I like table stakes. A betting limit just slows things down. But it's a fair-sized game."

"Can anybody walk in?"

"It depends."

"Will they let us in?"

"They know me," he said simply.

Casino Lupo was a stucco Spanish-style place, sprawling in the middle of three acres of neatly landscaped grounds. A Mexican kid parked the Olds. Marty led her up four steps to a door. A Mexican with a waxed moustache greeted Marty by name and led them inside. "Two hundred," he said, handing her a bundle of bills. "The cashier will sell you some chips. See what you can do."

"When will I see you?"

"A few hours. I'll be through that archway over there. Drop in if you run out of chips, or if you get bored."

She went to the cashier's window and bought a hundred dollars worth of chips. She went from there to the roulette wheel, stood watching for a few spins. Then she put a chip on Red. Black came up and the croupier took her chip away.

She played Red again and won. She left the two chips there and won again.

She had four chips now. She left one on Red, moved the other three to Low Third, numbers one through twelve. Seven-Black came up. She lost the chip on the Red but collected two-to-one on the other stack. She had nine chips now, and she bet five on Odd, four on Black. Seven came up again and she collected on both bets. Now she had eighteen chips. She played six each on 18, 4, and 23. The number was 4, the payoff 35-to-1. She now had 210 chips.

She went on playing. Her luck slowed down some but held. She let the wheel absorb her, let herself fall into the pattern of it. The ball whirled around, bounced from one number to another, dropped in a slot and stayed there. Men lost and other men won. Once she had a hundred dollars riding on Black and lost. She played fifty dollars on Low Third again and won. She let the chips stay where they were and won again.

It seemed no time at all when Marty was holding her arm. "Wait a minute," she said. "A few more plays."

"Three more," he said.

She lost twenty dollars playing Red, won thirty with a ten-dollar bet on one-through-nine, won twenty more playing Even.

He helped her carry her chips to the cashier's window. She found out, and was surprised to learn, that she had won twelve hundred dollars.

"In no time at all," she said.

"You've been playing for three hours."

"Really?"

"Really. Let's go get dinner."

"All right. How did you do?"

"I had lousy cards," he said. "I folded straight off on the first twelve pots."

"Did you lose?"

"No. I caught a few good hands and milked them, won fifty or sixty dollars. But I didn't go crazy the way you did. You'll make debauchery profitable."

She laughed.

They left the casino, went to his car. He tipped the attendant with a dollar chip. "Play a good number," he said. The boy smiled.

"Where to now?"

"Dinner," he said.

"In Paso?"

"In Juarez. The town isn't just tacos and tamales. There's a good steakhouse near the plaza. Can you eat a steak?"

"I could eat ten of them."

She only ate one. It was a top sirloin, charcoal broiled, burnt on the outside and raw in the middle. They had tequila with the meal and she went through the ritual with salt and lemon. It burned wildly but the jolt it gave you was nice. Between them, they killed a small bottle. She was nicely lit by the time they left the place.

"Now where?"

"Bernardo's," he said. "You sit next to me on a divan and we listen to guitars. Some mariachi music, too. We put down some more tequila and neck a little. Okay?"

"Fine."

They sat on a small sofa and killed most of another bottle of tequila. A boy brought a tray of sandwiches and she had some kind of hot sausage between two halves of a sesame seed roll. The music was soft and sensual. Marty kissed her, squeezed her breasts. Her head swam.

Then he was saying, "Had enough? Let's go somewhere else."

"Why?" She rubbed the back of his neck.

"Just to catch another scene."

"Can't we just stay here?"

Her other hand was rubbing his chest now.

"You'll like it there," he explained.

"Not as much as I like this."

She continued rubbing.

He put his hand on the hand she had on his chest.

"Let's go now, ah?"

"Back to your home? I'd like that,"

"No. Not right now anyway. We'll go someplace else first."

"Where?"

"A night club I know."

"Night clubs aren't so exciting."

"This one is," he said. "Good food and good drinks. And a good floorshow."

"I've seen floorshows."

"Not like this one."

"Oh," she said. "You mean they have a woman make it with a Shetland pony? That kind of thing?"

"That kind of thing. I don't know about Shetland ponies, but that's the general idea. They do it on stage."

"Let's go, Marty."

They left Bernardo's, found the Olds again. Marty unlocked the door, then changed his mind. "I don't want to park around there," he said. "The kid'll ruin the car."

He hailed a cab, helped her in. She leaned against him and moistened her lips with her tongue.

"Delia's Place," he told the driver.

CHAPTER FIVE

When Weaver woke, he bathed in the tub down the hall, then took his time combing his hair very carefully, plastering the long strands over his low forehead. He went to the dresser next, opened a drawer, pushed aside clothing until he found the straight razor. He carried it to the bed, sat upon the bed's edge, and opened the razor.

It was very sharp. He rubbed his thumb across the face of the blade, testing the sharpness, and smiled when he saw how keen the edge was. He held the weapon to the light and noted how the sides of the blade gleamed with newness, how the steel shone with a mirror's brilliance. Reluctantly, he closed the razor, pocketed it.

He breathed deeply, filling his lungs with air. His sleep that day, a clammy sort of sleep in a hot room, had been filled with dreams. Girls screamed in Weaver's sleep that day. Razors flashed and blood flowed. Twice he had awakened, his hands dampened with his own sweat, his heart pounding with hysterical excitement. Each time he had drifted back to Fantasyland, back to sleep, back to more screams and more razors and more blood.

Now he was ready.

He had selected his victim carefully. It would be simple this way and there would be a touch of beauty to the crime, an artistic element to the killing and rape. The girl he was going to murder was in the room next to his. That honey blonde, the one he'd met on his way to the can a day ago.

He saw her again now in his mind. He saw the lithe young

body, the thrusting breasts, the wriggling butt. Involuntarily his hand went to his pocket and trembling fingers sought out the razor. He opened it, stared at the gleam of the blade while the girl's image danced nude in his mind.

He saw the razor slashing, saw cruel red lines appear on the creamy breasts and the fleshy buttocks. He saw the girl's lips part for a shrill shriek. He saw himself upon her, his body between her thighs, his razor slashing those thighs to make them drip red blood.

Then him, surging into her. Then the culmination, and then a final desperate slash of the razor.

And death.

He was excited now, feverish. He closed the razor again with a snap, dropped it back into his pocket. He went to the door, twisted the knob, walked out into the hallway and moved to the door where he had seen the young blonde. He hesitated, his hand patting the razor in his pocket for reassurance. He knocked on the door, waited, and knocked again. There was no answer.

He knocked again, and again there was no response to his knocking. He thought that perhaps she was sleeping, and he knew that it would be even better that way, that he could gag her with a pillow slip and have her powerless before she was fully awake. Then he could take his time with her.

His hand found the doorknob, twisted it. The door was unlocked. He pushed it slowly open and stole into the room.

It was empty.

Disappointment flooded him. He closed the door and prowled the room, looking for her clothing, her personal effects. He found only a dirty white blouse in a wastebasket, and upon this garment he vented his fury. He slashed it a dozen times with the razor, gashing huge holes where the breasts would have been if the blouse had been occupied by its owner. He reduced the blouse to shreds and stuffed the shreds back in the wastebasket. Downstairs, he asked the clerk if the little blonde was still staying at the hotel.

"Guess not," the old man said. "Never checked out, but never paid for tonight. You never know with that kind. They're here again, there again. They travel light and leave with the morning mist. Don't trust 'em, myself. Young 'uns that travel alone. They're up to no good, I'd say."

She was gone, then.

Weaver went back to his room. It was cruel, he decided, cruel and unfair. He had primed himself for that one girl and now she was gone, free from him. It was not fair.

He washed his face with ice water, combed his hair again. He would have to find someone else, some other young thing with breasts and buttocks and a mouth made for the screams of terror. But it was too early yet, too early to seek out a victim on the city streets. Too many people were still awake.

He smiled. He could wait.

The night would be a long one. And, while the city slept, he would find another girl. He would rape her and hurt her and kill her, and all the nation would live in fear of him.

Marty looked around the club and wished he was as drunk as Meg was. Meg was stoned to the ears with tequila, and that was as it should be. But the juice hadn't reached Marty as well as it should have. He was still in control. That usually happened with him. He had the quick and sure control of the professional gambler, and it took a tremendous quantity of alcohol to throw this control off.

The headwaiter was a slender Mexican with oriental, almond-shaped eyes. He wore a black tuxedo that was a little too large for him. His shoes were black and pointed.

Marty found a ten dollar bill, folded it lengthwise and slapped it into the headwaiter's palm, and it disappeared quickly.

"I want a table up front," he said. "A good table."

"A very good table," said the Mexican. He was smiling.

"I want to be able to smell the sex," Marty said, "A ringside seat for the bouts. You got that?"

"*Si*," the Mexican said. "This way, please."

Marty stepped aside so that Meg could follow the Mexican. He walked behind her, letting his eyes give Delia's Place the once-over. The club was plush by Mexican standards, shabby by American ones. U.S. tourists filled the small tables. There was no floorshow yet, just a three-piece mariachi band, playing poorly, and the tourists talked volubly over the music and did a lot of heavy drinking. They were mostly men, but a few had women with them.

The table they wound up at was the best in the house, front and center, and just inches from the stage. There was a bed in the center of the stage, a large double bed with flat black sheets. Marty smiled; the black sheets were a good touch. They would make for nice contrast. White flesh and black sheets—a pretty picture.

"A bottle of your best tequila," he told the waiter who came to their table. "No food just now. The tequila is all."

"Tequila," the man said. He left to get it.

"Have you been here before?"

He looked at Meg. "Never,'" he said.

"I've heard about these places. I always wanted to go to one."

"I never got around to it before," he said. "It's a convenient set-up. You watch the show, if any of the performers appeals, you arrange to meet her in a back room for a half hour or so. First you watch and then you play games of your own."

"Will we do that?"

He shrugged. "If you want."

"I think I'd like that," she said. "To watch you make love to one of these whores. I'd like that."

"What would you like about it?"

"I don't know. It would be exciting, I think. I've made love with you, and first I'll watch somebody make love to one of the whores, and then I can watch you with the whore. Sort of a combination, I suppose."

"And then what? You want a man for yourself?"

"I've got you, Marty."

He laughed easily. "This is debauchery," he told her. "You can have all the men you want. I won't even be jealous."

"Not even a little?"

"Not even a little."

"I think maybe I'd rather you were a little jealous."

The waiter saved him the trouble of thinking up an answer to her last line. The man set a bottle of tequila on the table, placed a small glass in front of Meg and another in front of Marty. Marty opened the bottle and spilled two ounces of the colorless liquid into each glass. They touched glasses and tossed the stuff off.

"When does the show start?"

"Soon," he told her.

Almost as he said the word, the mariachi band finished their number, packed their instruments under their arms and found another house to haunt. The house lights went all the way out and the club was blackened like London during the Blitz. Then a spotlight—a golden green—shot out to illuminate the stage. There was a girl in the spot who had taken her place while lights were out.

Marty looked at her. She was a Mexican, her skin a golden brown, her hair short and dark. She smiled at the audience and her white teeth flashed. She was of medium height, with an hourglass figure. Most of the sand was still in the top half. Her breasts were huge, her waist slender, her hips round and just full enough.

"I wan' to welcome you to Delia's Place," she said. "I hope you have good time. Now do show start."

The girl was wearing a pale green dress which the spotlight set off nicely. Now a muted horn began to play somewhere, and the girl went into a clumsy but effective dance. She sashayed back and forth, letting the audience get a good look at her body. She reached in back with one hand and tugged a small string. The dress, designed for just such an occasion, promptly fell away to the floor of the stage.

She wore no underwear. Her bare body was the same golden brown hue all over, and her figure was perfect. Marty looked at the firm breasts, the tiny waist. He glanced across the table at Meg, who was watching the Mexican girl with breathless attention.

"Like her?" he asked.

"Shhh. This is interesting."

Marty chuckled, filled both their glasses with tequila. He downed his in a swallow but Meg didn't even pick up her glass. He set his down empty, looked again at the Mexican girl. She was holding her breasts in her own hands, bouncing them up and down. She pinched her own nipples and Marty watched them grow stiff in response to the self-administered stimulation. She reached lower and stroked her flat stomach, then reached lower still and began to caress herself, making small moans of simulated desire as she did so.

Meg's eyes were gleaming now, Marty saw. Meg was excited. He remembered how she had responded to the pictures. Evidently she liked vicarious kicks, he thought. She was all hot over the Mex girl.

The Mexican girl moaned once and then the spotlight died
and the room was dark again. Marty blinked in the dark. If that
was all there was to it, he thought, then Delia's Place was
picking its customers. But evidently it wasn't. The light went on
again—a white spot this time. Now a man had joined the girl.
The man was a Mexican, evidently in his middle twenties. He
had no clothes to remove, because he was already conveniently
naked.

The girl turned to face the man. She began to dance at him,
her breasts swaying, her hips twitching. The man let her come
closer. His hands reached out and accepted her breasts. He
fondled them and the girl writhed in his hands, moaning louder
and louder with desire.

Marty watched them, watched Meg as well. The horn—a
baritone sax, he decided—was still moaning along with the girl,
spinning out a gutbucket blues. Meg was entranced. He could
tell how hot she was. Plenty hot, he decided. Hot enough to
burn.

The man was holding the girl by her breasts now. She was
dancing backward, moving toward the bed. The man held onto
her breasts and moved with her. The backs of her thighs pressed
up against the bed. The man closed in. He let go of her breasts
and let his arms slip around her body. One hand held her by
her buttocks while the other was planted in the center of her
back: He kissed her, their mouths glued together, and her
breasts flattened against his sleek, hairless chest.

Marty could see the beads of sweat on their bodies. He could
almost feel the heat emanating from them.

Gently, the man pushed the girl backward. She lay on the
bed facing the audience with her head down on a pillow and
her feet still planted upon the floor of the stage. Her breasts
pointed up at the ceiling. The man stood in front of her with his

back to the audience. His hands reached again for her breasts. He held a nipple in each hand and began to rotate her nipples between his thumbs and forefingers. The girl moaned louder and louder and the sax wailed in the background.

Marty looked at Meg again. It wasn't hard to see how excited she was. She was handling herself now. With one hand she stimulated her own breasts. Her other hand was out of sight beneath the table. Marty grinned. He could guess what she was doing with it.

The Mex girl's thighs were parted now. The man stepped aside for a moment so that the audience could examine the girl. Then he resumed his place and stepped in closer. His hands gripped the girl's thighs, pressing them still further apart.

Then he began.

The girl on the black sheet writhed like a snake. Meg, too, was moaning. The girl's breasts heaved. Her feet left the floor and her long legs wound around the man's thighs, gripping him. Her hips churned, meeting his lust with her lust. The girl moaned, and the baritone sax moaned with her.

"Jesus," Lily said. "You'd think somebody was killing that broad. What's the matter with her?"

Cassie laughed. "That's Chita," she said, "Chita's the best groaner in the business. She can carry on like that when she don't feel a thing. With a trick, for example. She can make some stupid jerk think he's sending her like to the moon."

Lily didn't say anything. When Chita was finished it was going to be her turn. Not right away, of course; first the mariachi band would make some bad music for ten or fifteen minutes while waiters brought fresh drinks around and while men who were ready for action left to meet Chita or some of the other girls. Then, after the intermission was over, she and Cassie would be next on the program. She could tell that Cassie was hot just thinking about it. She herself was not. It was something of a kick to make it with Cassie, but making it privately was different than making it for an audience. Lily was fairly certain that the act was going to be an act all the way as far as she herself was concerned. She would do what she was supposed to do, and she would lie there while Cassie did her part, but she didn't expect to get much of a bang out of the whole thing. It would be boring as hell.

"You got to give Ringo credit," Cassie was saying now. "The way he has that horn grooving in the background, picking up Chita's moans and cooking along with her. That's the whole bit about this type of scene, Lily. What they do on the stage is nothing. It's the extra little kicks you can supply so the guy watching thinks he's seeing something different."

"Solid."

"You got to make like a production out of it, Lily. The little extra kicks make it special. I mean, a guy may wig just seeing another guy slipping it to a chick. But it's a bigger kick when they do something far out, or when they do it with bells ringing."

"I'm hip," Lily said. She was getting into her costume now, a frilly little-girl dress, pink and white and ruffled.

"Take that dress," Cassie said. "Another good idea of Ringo's. It makes you look about twelve years old, and you've got a baby face to go with it. The figure is no baby shape, but that's okay as it is. It's hot enough for a cat to watch two chicks grooving together, but it gets even hotter when one of them looks like a kid. Get it?"

"Got it."

"I could tell you something," Cassie went on. "Something that would have old Ringo squirming in his pants if he knew about it. You know that cat up there with Chita? The cat she's doing all the moaning about?"

"I don't know his name."

"His name's Pancho. And this'll bust you up, Lily. He's Chita's brother."

"What?"

Cassie's eyes sparkled. "Her brother, Lily. I swear to God. One night Chita got smashed on tequila and put me hip. She told me he was the first guy who ever made it with her, when she was twelve and he was fourteen. He caught her while she was taking a bath and he copped her cherry before she knew what it was all about. They've been making it ever since. She takes all the tricks she can handle, but Pancho's the only cat who ever gets her for free."

"I suppose they want to keep it in the family."

"I don't know what it is, but that's how it swings. And if Ringo knew about it, you can bet he'd put the audience wise. Can you imagine watching a chick making it with her brother?"

"If that's her kick," Lily said, "then more power to her. But why in hell did she stop moaning? Are they done?"

"They're not done."

"So why no moans and groans?"

"Because they're doing it another way," Cassie said, a silly smile on her thin face. "And she can't moan now, Lily. It's impossible."

Meg was still shaking. Her body ached dully with desire and throbbed with need. The house lights were on now, and the waiter was bringing them a fresh bottle of tequila, and the same intrepid trio was playing mariachi music. But Meg's mind still whirled with the memory of the Mexican guy and the Mexican gal, loving like savages in the spotlight just a few yards away.

There had been a moment when she had almost left her chair, had very nearly torn off her own clothing and leaped onto the stage to join in the fun. She had wanted to throw herself upon the contorted bodies on the bed, had wanted to add her own sweat to the pool of perspiration upon the black sheet. But she had controlled herself until the impulse passed.

She looked at Marty. It was strange—she was very highly sexed-up now, so much so that she felt ready to explode, but still she had no immediate desire to make love to Marty. He was a perfect lover and the whole night long had never failed to excite her. But now she was more concerned with a different sort of excitement. The show was driving her mad, not because she needed a man's embrace but because it was so exotic, so forbidden. There was a genuinely evil aspect to it, and this sense of evil was driving her wild.

Now Marty was sniffing the air, a bemused expression on his face. "That smell," he said. "Do you recognize it?"

"No."

"Ever smoke marijuana?"

"Never."

"That's what it is," he told her. "And somebody's smoking one whole hell of a lot of it."

"Isn't it illegal in Mexico?"

"Sure, but so's prostitution. Like to try some?"

"I don't know. What will it do to me?"

"Probably knock you on your ear. Not like alcohol. You won't pass out. You'll just get higher and higher."

She was already wonderfully high, but she wanted more, more of everything. She told him to get some and he called the waiter over to the table.

"Marijuana," he said. "Four or five cigarettes."

When the waiter came back, leaving five slender brown cigarettes with twisted ends on the table, Marty handed one to her and put another between his own lips. He lit them both and she took a drag of hers. It tasted a little like a Turkish cigarette she had smoked once. She did not particularly like or dislike the taste.

"Hold the smoke in your lungs longer," Marty suggested.

"Why?"

"So you absorb it into your bloodstream. That's what gets you high. The more you get into your blood, the higher you get and the faster you get there. Just hold it as long as you can."

Meg closed her eyes and smoked. On the first try, she coughed almost immediately upon inhaling and lost the bulk of the smoke. After that she began to get the hang of it.

It was working before she realized it. She finished the first cigarette and used Marty's lighter to start a second. Midway through the second, she realized that her head was light, that colors were brighter than before, that the mariachi music sounded good for the first time. Marty said something to her, something very trivial, and it seemed hysterically funny. She started to laugh and could not stop. She simply went on laughing until she was gasping for breath.

"Marty."

"What, baby?"

"I'm high, Marty."

"I know."

"Are you high?"

"I'm getting an edge on."

"I'm so high, Marty. And so *hot!*" That, she thought, was certainly the truth. She was so hot she was going to set the whole night club on fire. Instead of calming her sexual urges, the marijuana had made her realize just how excited she was. She closed her eyes and felt the blood flowing in her loins, felt the warmth that flooded her big breasts.

So hot. She spilled tequila into her glass and drank it right down. It settled in her stomach. She let her eyes close again and felt the warmth of the Mexican firewater in her belly.

"When does the show start again, Marty?"

"Soon, baby."

"Good."

He stood up now, moved his chair so that he was sitting next to her instead of across from her. He put his arm around her shoulder. She took his hand and positioned it on her breast. His fingers flexed and she shivered, her blood pounding through her veins. She took his other hand and wedged it up under her dress.

His hand moved further upward, he caressed her and she sobbed.

"Warm," he said.

"Play with me, Marty. Oh, God!"

There was no moon. Clouds masked the stars. It was night, a dark night, and it was time to begin.

Weaver left the hotel without speaking to the old man behind the desk. He walked through the streets, detoured through darker alleyways. It was still a little too early, he thought, because there were still too many people on the streets, too much automobile traffic. Still, it was time to begin, time to search. His first victim, the girl in Tulsa, had been an accident of fate. She had blundered across his path. But there was no reason to assume that he would be that lucky again.

He couldn't wait for the next one to come to him. He would have to seek her out, whoever she might be, wherever she was now. He would have to find her and stalk her, and when the time was right he would strike like a black panther in the night, like a vampire.

On Perry Street, not far from his hotel, he wandered into a

bar. It was a skid row sort of place with a strong beer and urine smell. The television set was on, tuned in on an old Gary Cooper western. Three wine drinkers held up one end of the bar. A woman, a little drunk and a little slutty, sat at the far end. She turned when Weaver came in, and she flashed him a professionally brilliant smile.

He avoided her at first, walking to the middle of the bar and asking for a glass of draft beer. The bartender drew a beer for him and he took a sip. He had never especially cared for the taste of beer. He did not especially care for it now.

"Hey," the woman called. "Come here, Mac."

He turned and really looked at her for the first time. She was somewhere in her thirties but it was hard to tell just where. The liquor she had been drinking hid her age neatly enough; she could have been thirty or forty or anywhere in between. Her hair was dark brown, her mouth painted with a great deal of lipstick. Her breasts were large and heavy.

She called to him again. This time he went over to her, carrying his glass of beer with him. He set the beer down on the top of the bar and seated himself upon the stool at her side.

"You look like a nice guy," she said. "Minute you came in, I said to myself, there's a nice guy."

He did not answer her. He was sizing her up now, trying to decide whether or not she would do. Actually, he thought, she was too old. He would have preferred a young girl, someone around the age of the honey blonde he had seen at the hotel. But the blonde was gone. He couldn't have the blonde tonight, and this woman was presenting herself, ready for the razor. She would be easy.

"Want to buy me a drink?"

He signaled the bartender. The woman was drinking rye and ginger ale. The bartender poured a shot of rye, filled a water tumbler halfway with ginger ale, dropped in a pair of ice cubes, and poured the shot in. He stirred the drink with a plastic swizzle stick and gave it to the woman. Weaver paid for the drink.

"Here's to a hell of a nice guy," the woman said. She raised her glass and nodded her head slightly at Weaver, then sipped her drink. She put the glass down and put her hand on Weaver's thigh. She patted him gently and smiled at him.

"You want to know something," she said. "You want to know something. I like you. I honest to God like you. Minute you came through that door, I said to myself, I like that guy."

"That's nice," Weaver said.

"I'm not kidding, either."

"Good."

Her hand stroked his thigh. "My name is Audrey," she told him. "You got a name?"

"Mac," he said. "You got it right before."

"You mean it? Your name's Mac?"

"That's right," Weaver said. "Mac Johnson."

"No kidding," Audrey said. Her hand, working cleverly, stole inside. She touched him and his own hand went at once to his pocket. He held the razor in his hand, clutching it for support.

"Mac," she said, "I got a swell idea. Why should we pay bar prices for liquor? Instead we can go up to my room. I got a bottle there and we can drink for nothing."

He didn't answer for a moment. She touched him, skillfully and excitingly, and his grip was tighter on the razor.

The razor. The razor.

He pictured it in his mind, bright and shiny.

The blade flashed in his mind.

Flash.

Flash.

Flash.

Suddenly the white flash of the razor blade became the white roundness of her breasts.

A white circle.

Then the white circle of her breasts became the moon.

The moon grew in size and got larger and larger.

Then the color of the moon changed. It became a harvest moon as the white changed to yellow and the yellow changed to orange.

Then the orange became red.

Red.

Bright red.

Bright blood red, and the red began to drip off of the moon.

Drip.

Drip.

The blood had all run off now and the moon was white again.

He stared at it.

Stared and stared.

Stared so hard the white moon became two white moons.

He blinked and the moons became her white breasts.

A voice.

A voice had spoken to him.

He blinked again and looked up at the face.

It was a moon and he talked to it.

"That's a good idea," he said. "Let's go, Audrey."

Ringo took a cigar from his breast pocket, bit off the end, spat, put the cigar between his lips, and lit it.

A good crowd tonight, he thought. A good hot crowd watching a good hot show. Chita and Pancho had gone over nicely, especially the finale, which always got a rise out of the house. And Chita had received a healthy play during the intermission. The suckers were paying through their noses.

Ringo chewed his cigar. The intermission was just about over now. Time for Cassie and the new broad to do their stuff. He wondered how it would go over. Probably pretty well, he decided.

He walked to the dressing room, knocked on the door.

"Girls," he cooed, "you're on."

CHAPTER SIX

When the house lights dimmed rapidly to black, Lily hurried to take her place upon the stage. A Mexican stagehand was busy rearranging props and he patted her playfully on the behind while he worked. She ignored him and moved to the proper position. The pale red spot hit her directly and she went into her routine at once.

The stagehand placed a coat-rack by the side of the bed. Lily stood near it, smiled daintily and innocently at the audience. She made a small-girl curtsy. Then, with disarming nonchalance, she removed the pink and white dress. She took her time disrobing, but there was no suggestion of a strip-tease in the performance. She was simply a young girl undressing for bed.

Under the dress she wore a pale red bra and matching panties. Her underwear was just right for the particular spotlight focused upon her. She gathered up her dress, hung it neatly upon the coat-rack. She removed the bra with her back to the audience and hung it with the dress. She turned slowly, revealing her large firm breasts to the audience. Her hands stroked her breasts carelessly, then dropped to the elastic waistband of the red panties. She pushed the panties down and stepped out of them. She put them, also, on the rack, and once again she caressed herself with the casualness of a child.

Quite a production, she thought. If she had known she had such a load of acting ability, she would have gone down to L.A. with Jodi Wells to try out for the Playhouse. Hell, you'd think the cats out front would be happy enough just watching a little sex. But they had to have drama with it, for Christ's sake!

Naked now, she knelt at the side of the black-sheeted bed. She folded her hands on the sheet. She lowered her head and stared with amusement at her breasts, which pointed prettily at the floor of the stage. In a clear, childish voice she piped

> *Now I lay me down to sleep*
> *I pray the Lord my soul to keep*
> *If I should die before I wake*
> *I pray the Lord my soul to take.*

Too much, she thought. They even had to drag God into the act. She wondered which of Ringo or Cassie had written the script for the goddamn show. Maybe, if it went over big in Juarez, they would take the show next to Broadway. Maybe they'd even sell film rights.

A collective gasp from the audience let Lily know that Cassie was on the stage. The redhead came out behind her, stark naked, while Lily remained in praying position at the side of the bed. Cassie moved closer, until Lily felt the redhead's hands touch the back of her neck, stroking tenderly. Still she herself did not move. She breathed deeply and held her position while Cassie's hands travelled over her back, massaging her shoulder blades, coursing over her back until they cupped her plump buttocks.

Cassie fondled her buttocks, flexed them. Her fingers probed, and Lily began to feel the initial stirrings of excitement in spite of herself. Cassie was a skilled technician, an accomplished little dyke. She knew what to do and how to do it, and it worked.

Besides, Lily thought, there was a certain amount of kick in knowing you had an audience. A little power, like. All those cats were out there, getting horny as hell just watching her, and she was grooving on stage and driving them out of their heads. No, it wasn't bad at all. It was a brand new kind of kick.

Now Cassie's hands moved again, slipping to Lily's waist,

moving upward to grasp Lily's pendant breasts. The redheaded girl was bending over now and her own tiny breasts brushed up against Lily's back. When Cassie gripped her nipples and tugged at them, Lily let out the little moan that the script called for. And it wasn't just a matter of sticking to the script. She was getting warm as hell.

"Hello, little girl," Cassie said.

"Hello," she answered.

"I'm going to do things to you, little virgin. I'm going to have fun with you."

"I'm afraid," Lily said; that was supposed to make her seem more like a child, to introduce a hotter element into the game. Cassie didn't say anything now but went on caressing her breasts. Her fingers made circles around the pale tan aureoles which surrounded Lily's pink nipples. Next, Cassie put the tip of each index finger to a nipple and pressed as though she was ringing a doorbell.

Ding-a-ling-a-ling, Lily thought.

Cassie's hands caught the undersides of Lily's breasts and hoisted them. Lily moved forward, clambering onto the bed, her back still to the red-haired, flat-chested girl. Lily felt Cassie's hands on the backs of her thighs, stroking them gently and tenderly. After a few seconds of this, she rolled over onto her back, her legs extended toward the audience. There was a black pillow beneath her head and she spread her silky blonde hair over it with one hand while she rubbed her own stomach with the other.

Cassie joined her on the bed, leaping over, brushing Lily's lips with a quick kiss. Still Lily played her part—the pure and innocent little thing, enduring caresses without responding. She lay motionless while Cassie continued to work on her breasts.

Staying motionless now was not especially simple. Cassie

licked her breasts with a warm tongue, moving in on the nipples, tormenting the soft skin with sensuous caresses. Then Cassie caught a nipple between her bloodless lips and sucked hard on it. A rush of excitement shot through Lily's body, a flood of warmth that made it hellishly difficult to stay still.

To hell with the script, she thought. She put one hand on the nape of Cassie's neck and fondled the redhead there, pressing Cassie's face hard against her breast. She felt one of Cassie's hands, high on the inside of her thigh.

Lily wondered how the audience felt now. Chita and her brother Pancho had given everybody one hell of a jolt, and all they'd shown was some fairly straight man–woman sex. But this was lesbianism, and with a twist—one of the actresses was playing the part of a child.

I'll bet they're going nuts, she thought. I'll bet we get a hell of a lot of business tonight. Every stud in Juarez would be heading for her room.

She smiled secretly. Cassie was kissing her other breast now, working on it like a maniac. And all Lily could think was that she was going to have hit that Ringo cat for a raise.

Audrey looked better in the dark. She was holding Weaver's arm now as they walked along Perry Street, heading away from the bar where he had picked her up. Now, out of the glare of the lights, her face was softer, her age several years less in appearance. She wasn't perfect, he thought. But you couldn't expect to get a perfect one every time out. You had to settle for what you could find.

"Nice night, Mac. Don't you think?"

He didn't answer her. His right hand still held the razor. He was trying to decide where to do it. The streets were dark enough, but it was still too early to count on safety from an interruption. She had said they would go to her room. Well, maybe that was the best idea. He could wait, and have his fun in her room.

Yes, that would be better.

"Something the matter, Mac?"

"No, nothing's the matter."

"You don't talk much."

To reassure her, he put his left arm around her shoulder and gave her a hug. Still, though, his right hand held onto the razor. It was as though the razor was the essence of his maleness and he was terrified to be caught without it.

"I live just the next block," Audrey said. "It ain't much. Just a lousy room on the third floor."

"Is it quiet?"

"Sure it is."

"And private?"

"Oh, I'll say it's private," she said. She giggled. "Don't you worry about a thing on that scope, Mr. Mac Johnson. It's as private as you could want it. We won't have no interruptions."

That was important, he thought. She had no idea how important it was. He looked at her now, thinking what a sloppy thing she was, and it suddenly occurred to him that he was doing her a tremendous favor. What was she, anyway? Just a no-account tramp who would never amount to a thing. She was a nobody, just as he himself had been before he killed the girl in Tulsa.

But now she would be important. Now, because of what he was going to do to her, Audrey would have her name and picture in all the papers. She would be a somebody, not so important as Weaver, maybe, but a damn sight more important than she was now.

He smiled.

"Something funny, Mac?"

"I was just thinking."

"What?"

"That I like you," he said. "That you and me'll have a good time."

This seemed to please her. She stopped in front of a three-story frame building with a sign out front advertising rooms for rent. The front door was ajar. He walked inside with her and followed her up two flights of creaking stairs to her room on the third floor. Once inside, he saw that the place she lived in managed to make Cappy's look like the Ritz. The double bed sagged and the dresser was ready to fall apart. She didn't even have a fan, for God's sake.

He decided it was a shame a woman had to live like this. Well, he would be doing her a favor, all right. There were no two ways about it. He would be taking her away from this hovel, from a life of bringing home men to stay alive. And at the same time he would be making her famous, putting her picture and story in the newspapers so everybody could feel sorry for her. He was doing her a real favor.

She turned to him, waiting to be kissed. He didn't want to kiss her but he did anyhow, so she wouldn't get suspicious. Then she took a slight step backward and gave him a huge smile.

"Mac," she said, "I hate to ask you. But could you spare about ten bucks? Reason I ask is I'm broke. I hate to ask."

Five, be thought, would be about right. But what difference did it make how much he gave her? He could take the money back, along with whatever money she had around the dingy room. So he took out his wallet, found two fives and gave them to her. "You're a sport, Mac. Thanks." He watched her put the two bills in her top dresser drawer. Then she smiled again, and then she took off her clothes. He just plain stood there while she took everything off. She didn't have a bad shape, he had to admit. Her breasts hung down a little but there was a lot of nice flesh there. And her legs were still good.

"Well, come on, Mac."

He said, "You forgot something."

"What?"

Smiling, he pointed behind her. She looked around, no doubt wondering what she had forgotten. And, with all his strength, he struck her on the back of the head.

The first blow only drove her to her knees, but when he hit her a second time she went down like a tree in the forest, with a crash.

She was a big woman but he was strong that night. He got her on top of the bed, on her back. With his razor he cut her dress to strips. He used the strips to tie each hand and each foot to a corner of the bed. When she was neatly spread-eagled he cut a fifth piece of cloth and gagged her so that she could not utter a sound.

Then he took off all his own clothing. He held the razor in his hand, a smile on his lips. He had not hit so terribly hard. She would come to very shortly.

Then he could begin.

Cassie was shaking like a leaf. Lily lay on the black sheets before her, her blonde hair brilliant on the glossy black pillow, her eyes closed, her breasts gleaming with the moisture of a few million tongue-kisses. Cassie stared at her, her own heart beating wildly.

Men had never meant much to her. She had lied slightly to Lily, telling the blonde girl that she was bisexual, that men and women gave her an equal charge. It didn't work that way. Men were something you put up with, something you balled with strictly for bread. That was why the show had always dragged her. She didn't mind making it with a man for money, in a room with the door closed. But she hated like hell to ball a guy with other studs watching. It seemed dirty.

This, strangely, did not. Now, when she was making love to Lily, all the men and women in the audience seemed to disappear entirely; she was alone with Lily, and Lily thrilled her tremendously. Her excitement at this moment, with a whole room full of people staring at her, was greater than when she had been with Lily in the privacy of their hotel room.

Again her hands reached out, holding Lily's breasts and playing with them.

Then, her hands still on those perfect chunky breasts, she let her body slip down from the bed a little. Her mouth was now level with Lily's belly. She continued caressing the blonde's breasts while her lips darted out to glide like a serpent over Lily's belly. She kissed the indentation that was Lily's navel. She rubbed her cheeks against Lily. And, all the while, her hands were busy.

Lily was hers now. Lily loved what she did to her and Lily liked to do it back to Cassie, and it was perfect. Cassie remembered how it had been with Didi, before Didi took up with Paul. It had been fine, they lived together and balled all the time and it was like heaven. Then that mother Paul had to come on and turn Didi straight again.

Well, that wouldn't happen with Lily. Lily was all hers and she was going to stay that way. She was what Cassie wanted, and the redhead would kill any man that went near her. Except for the paying tricks, of course. They would both take on men for bread, and they would take on each other for the fun of it. And they would groove.

She moved lower now. Her pulse raced and her blood pounded.

Here we go, she thought. Around the motherloving moon and straight into orbit.

✿

It was like the picture, Meg thought. It was like the picture, the one that showed the two lesbians. Except that it was better than the picture, because the picture was black-and-white and this was in living color. The picture was a still shot and this was action, terrifyingly vivid action. The picture was small, four inches by five inches, while this was larger than life, going on right before her eyes. It was better, much better, than any picture could possibly be. It was Cinemascope and 3-D and Cinerama and Vistavision and stereophonic sound, even Aromarama. It was, in short, phenomenally exciting, and she was phenomenally excited, to put it very mildly.

The redhead—the one who was doing everything to the blonde. Meg looked at the redhead and her mouth watered. She watched the redhead's hands, the redhead's lips.

Not a very well-constructed girl, that redhead. Almost hipless, and even more than almost breastless, with scrawny shanks and hollow eyes. And yet there was something compelling about the redhead, and something very very compelling about what the redhead was doing to the blonde.

The blonde, now—the blonde was beautiful, simply beautiful, and on that point there was no question at all in Meg Rector's mind. The blonde had a baby face and big-girl breasts and huggable hips. The blonde was lovely, and Meg watched what the redhead was doing to her and began to quiver more fiercely than ever.

She was high now, high up in the air, high with tequila and marijuana and sexual excitement. And Marty was next to her as high as she was, his hands hot flames searing her body. She grabbed him, held him, touched him. She put a hand to his face and stared into his eyes.

"Marty."

"What?"

"What she's doing," she said. "What that girl is doing to that other girl. What she's doing, up there."

"What about it?"

"Do it to me."

"Now?"

"Now."

"Later," he said, dreamily. "Not now."

"Now! Now, so I can watch it and feel it all at once. Now, damn it. Now, Marty!"

She said this last batch of sentences without looking at him. She was watching the redhead and the blonde now. The blonde had reversed her position on the bed, and her face was now at the foot of the bed near where Meg was seated. The redhead had moved, too, and was lying further up on the bed. The redhead's legs extended past the top of the blonde's head.

Meg knew what was going to happen next.

"Now, Marty. Please!"

He did not argue with her. He left his chair and slipped under the table, kneeling like a slave in front of her. She felt his hands slip under her skirt, finding her panties and pulling them downward over her legs and off, leaving them bunched on the floor. She felt him come to her, close to her, and all the while she watched the blonde and the redhead.

They were doing it now. And Marty was too.

Slowly, Ringo turned from the doorway and walked into the rear of the club. He plucked the cigar from between his teeth and glanced at it. He had chewed it almost to ribbons. He dropped it onto the floor now and ground it out beneath his heel.

A club like this, he thought, and you see plenty. A club like this is more than tossing out drunks from a 52nd Street strip joint or pimping for a stable of cows on the West Side. A club like this is all the way out and no holds barred.

But it still got to you, he thought. You saw everything in the world, night after goddamn night, and still, once in a while, it got to you. This happened rarely. But when it happened, the force of it was undeniable. Then you had to ease the tension or flip entirely.

Tonight it had gotten to him. Tonight, watching the new act, his loins had begun to burn and his heart had begun to race in his chest. The new girl, Lily. The redhead, Cassie. The two of them, going at it hotter than the Chicago fire and more turbulently than the Frisco quake. It got to him, all right. It knocked him on his ear.

Ringo was the perfect choice to head a club like Delia's. A lecher would have been bad business. A man who played around with the whores would, to coin a phrase, be eating up all the profits. And, to coin another phrase, he would be screwing up the normal routine. Fortunately Ringo was not that type of manager. He let the girls alone. He never propositioned them, never made sex a prerequisite to keeping their jobs. They put out for the customers and that was it. They didn't have to put out for Ringo, too.

Now he walked to a door, knocked on it. "It's Ringo," he said. "Open the goddamn door."

The door opened. Ringo stepped inside, closed it behind him. There was a hook-and-eye lock and Ringo dropped the hook into the eye. He did not intend to be interrupted.

"You did fine, kid," he said. "You were great. They loved you."
Pancho said nothing.

"Come on, Pancho," Ringo said. "It's time to be a good boy now. Get your clothes off."

Ringo watched, pleased, while the young Mexican removed

his clothes. Ringo's eyes traveled over Pancho's body. Ringo smiled. He unbelted his own pants and let them drop to the floor.

He said, "You don't like this, do you, Pancho?"

"I don't min'."

"The hell you don't mind. You hate it, you stupid little Mex. You can't stand it."

"I don't min'."

"Sure," Ringo said. "Turn around, Pancho."

Pancho turned around, turned his back to the manager of Delia's Place. Ringo looked at him, studied the smooth contours of his young masculine body. Ringo's smile spread. He stepped closer, his eyes bright.

"Now bend over," he said.

First, Audrey groaned. Then, while Weaver moved closer to the edge of the bed, her eyes opened. She saw Weaver, saw the razor in his hand. The razor was open now and Weaver's thumb moved back and forth across the face of the blade. Audrey tried to scream but no sound came through the gag. She tried to lurch free but the bonds held her securely in place, spread-eagled across the sagging bed.

Weaver said, "I'm going to kill you, Audrey. I'm going to cut you and hurt you and kill you."

Her eyes bugged in terror. He looked at her, delighted with her expression of fear. This was good, he thought. This was as it should be. Pure terror, naked fear, horrible horror. This was what they wanted in the movies, what they were getting at in the comic books. This was life.

But where to begin? Where to start?

He stood next to her, holding the razor tightly. Her chest heaved and he watched her breasts bob. That was a starting place, he thought. Those great big sagging breasts. A perfect place to start.

The razor was very sharp. It slipped neatly into the underside of one breast, slicing easily through Audrey's flesh. A thin trickle of blood flowed from the wound. Audrey screamed in silence against the gag and her whole body twisted with pain.

It was the blood that did it. Weaver stared at the blood and something happened. He was an animal now, a beast. The cool emotionless part of him vanished. He threw himself upon the woman, whipping at the sides of her body with the razor while he drove himself deep into her. He lay on top of her, drove savagely into her, then raised himself on one arm so that he could flail at her breasts with the razor.

Soon both breasts were criss-crossed with cruel cuts that bled freely. He put down the razor and gripped the bleeding breasts with his hands, flexing them while he rode her with the full force of his passion. It did not take him long to reach fulfillment. His passion came quickly and was soon spent. He lay for a moment, still holding tightly to her slashed breasts. Then, shakily, he got to his feet.

She was still alive, still conscious. And Weaver was by no means through. The sexual part was over and done with. He had taken the woman, had had his pleasure with her, and he would not need to make love to her again. But he had not finished hurting her. He had a marvelous opportunity here. She was helpless, unable to cry out and unable to fight back. They were alone and they would not be disturbed.

He could take his time.

He found a pack of matches in her dresser drawer, along with the two five dollar bills he had given her and three or four singles of her own. He lit a match, let it burn for a moment, and then dropped it onto her bare belly. It lay there for several seconds, flaming, until it burned itself out. He did this again, with another match.

There had been a movie that he remembered now. A movie

about the Great Fire of London. There had been a scene in which a woman ran through the streets of the city, her hair flaming. The woman had screamed nicely.

He looked at Audrey's hair. He wanted to set it on fire, but he was afraid that the fire would rage out of control and start the whole building aflame. Then another idea came to him. He lit another match and dropped it between her plump thighs. It burned for a long time there.

Audrey passed out this time. He waited patiently until her eyes opened once more, and then he went on.

When he left, finally, all of her body was scarred from matches. All her fingers and toes had been hacked off—he was pleased that the razor was made of such well-tempered steel. Her whole mattress was a pool of blood, and there were deep gashes in every part of her body.

Before he went out of the room he did several things. He washed at her washbowl, getting all the blood from his body. He dressed. And then, finally, he dipped the fingers of both hands into her blood and pressed all ten fingers to the wall, over her bed.

He wanted them to know he killed Audrey. He wanted the credit. He wanted El Paso to know that there was a fiend in its midst, and that the fiend bore the name of Michael Patrick Weaver.

Outside, the night was cool and clear. It was around four in the morning and the streets were deserted. Weaver walked around aimlessly for ten or fifteen minutes taking the fresh night air into his lungs, walking far from the three-story frame building where Audrey's corpse lay attracting flies. He felt no guilt, no remorse.

On the contrary, he was flushed with pride. This had been

no accident, like the time in Tulsa. This had been carefully planned and carefully executed. This had been perfect, from beginning to end.

He started back to his hotel, and was halfway there before he realized what a stupid thing such a course of action would be. The police were going to find those fingerprints instantly. In a matter of hours they would know that Weaver was the killer. And his picture was in the files, so it would be in the El Paso evening paper. If he was still asleep at his hotel, they would have him under arrest before he opened his eyes.

And they would take him to headquarters, and they would beat him. It was only reasonable to assume that the El Paso police beat you the way the Tulsa police had done once. They would beat him, and try him for murder, and put him in the electric chair to smell his own flesh burning. He had smelled burning flesh already that night. Audrey's flesh. He did not want to smell his own flesh when the electrical current seared through it.

His mind worked quickly. A day or two ago, he had been unwillingly to try sneaking across the border. Then it seemed easier to stay in El Paso, to wait for capture, to stay holed up and wait until they smoked him out. But now it was different. Now, for one thing, he was an active panther rather than a passive rabbit. Besides, if he was going to stay alive, he just plain had to get across the border. He was a sitting duck in El Paso. In Juarez he might have a chance.

In a day, when Audrey's broken body had been discovered and when his own bloody prints had been identified, all the border guards would be on the lookout for him. Now he was still an unknown in El Paso, a Tulsa fugitive who could be anywhere. If he was going to make it to Juarez, now was the time to get going.

He pictured himself going across the border.

The guard stepping out of the guard house.

First glancing at him.

Then staring.

Then recognizing him.

It's Weaver!

It's Michael Patrick Weaver!

He saw himself running, running across the border.

Pushing aside people—screaming people.

The people lined up and let him pass.

They all chanted his name.

Michael Patrick Weaver.

Michael Patrick Weaver.

Michael Patrick Weaver.

They all knew him.

They all recognized turn.

He felt proud as he ran across the border.

Then he heard shots ring out from behind him.

Zing!—the bullets flew past him.

Then one hit him—and another.

But he kept on running and running.

They couldn't stop him.

He was Michael Patrick Weaver.

And he ran and he ran. The ground flew fast beneath him, so fast that suddenly he was no longer on the ground but was in the air.

He was flying through the air. He was Superman. Then he dove into an ocean beneath him and skimmed through the water. He was Submariner.

He got into a car—tired, wanting to ride. And as he roared away deep into Mexico he was the Green Hornet.

He stopped the car and got out.

He was Michael Patrick Weaver again.

He walked toward the border, nervous inside, on the verge of panic. But when he got there it turned out to be much easier than he had imagined. The border was barely guarded at all. A uniformed officer looked him over, but did not recognize him or see anything suspicious. Weaver stepped over a line, and Weaver was in Mexico, and nothing could have been easier.

He found a hotel in Juarez, a cheap rundown hotel that was half inn and half brothel. He paid a dollar for a room and was shown to a bug-trap similar to his place at Cappy's, except that there was not even a washbowl here.

He had to go down the hall to comb his flat black hair over his low forehead. He did this, and then he went back to his room, turned on the overhead fan and went to sleep.

CHAPTER SEVEN

In the morning it was raining. The rain was the first thing Marty was aware of. Rain lashed the bedroom windows, spilled in through the screens. The rain was coming down hard and the noise it made was not a gentle one. Rain was a rare commodity in El Paso, especially during the summer. So Marty noticed it before anything else. He lay on his back, on his bed, and he listened to the rain.

After the fact of the rain, other facts came home to him. The fact that his head was being torn into several pieces by a sharp, insistent pain that began somewhere in the back of his skull. The fact that his skin was covered with clammy sweat, that he was dizzy and nauseous. The fact that it was morning, that he was at home in his own bed in his own bedroom. The fact that Meg was with him, also in the bed, and still asleep.

These facts brought with them a rush of memories. Memories of the casino where he had played poker while Meg won twelve or thirteen hundred dollars at the roulette wheel. Memories of dinner, memories of a night club with soft music and too much tequila. Memories of another night club, Delia's Place. Memories of the floor show, of the marijuana, of more of the floor show, of sex with Meg. Memories of afterward, of himself in a small room making love to a Mexican whore while Meg stood at their side, watching and applauding.

The memories ceased at that point in time. At some indeterminate point afterward he had evidently herded the big brunette into the Olds and had somehow driven the Olds back across the border to his house. God alone knew how this had happened.

Marty remembered nothing, and could only guess that the Olds had taken over the driving for him. After the tequila and the marijuana and the sex, it seemed less than likely that he could have handled the driving all by himself.

He managed to get up onto an elbow. He looked at Meg, and his mouth curled in distaste, though whether directed at her or at himself he couldn't have said. Both, probably. The last time he'd woken up with her he'd loved the sight of her, the fact of her. The idea of sharing a night of debauchery with a girl as eager for it as he was. But this time, in the cold light of a rainy morning, things looked different. It wasn't just the hangover that was turning his stomach. Had that been him, kneeling on the dirty floor between her legs? And had that been her, urging him on?

She was sleeping on her back now, breathing through her open mouth. The sweat was a visible film on her body, as it was on his. Her body odor—sweat smells and sex smells and alcoholic smells—was strong and unpleasant.

A pig, he thought bitterly. It felt better to lash out than to look within. A pig with money and taste and a nice shape, a pig who played good bedtime games. A pig who could talk, intelligently. But still just as much of a pig.

He remembered the way she had behaved at Delia's, the way she had acted in the room afterward. A pig in the rutting season, he thought. And then he remembered the way he himself had acted. Fine, he thought. I'm a pig, too. That doesn't mean I have to share my sty with her. One pig doesn't have to like another pig just because they've been eating slops together out of the same trough. No law says so.

He swung his legs over the side of the bed and sat up. His headache was more acute now and his whole head was splitting with the pain. He got to his feet and his stomach started to turn over. He got to the john, closed the door, and threw up into the toilet bowl. He flushed the toilet, found a bottle of aspirin tablets in the medicine cabinet, spilled three into the palm of his left hand, filled the plastic water tumbler with three inches of tap water, and swallowed the aspirin. When the pills and water hit bottom he had to resist the impulse to heave them up again. He took a deep breath, held it, let it out. He breathed again, deeply, and exhaled.

The headache was still there. In the television ads they showed you how the aspirins dissolved into millions of tiny specks the second you swallowed them, and how those specks forced their way into your bloodstream, and how your headache was gone in no time at all. It didn't work that way. He sat down on the toilet, resting his head in the palm of one hand.

He wasn't used to headaches. Generally he awoke with a perfectly clear head, with his mind in flawless working order. He didn't like to wake up with clammy sweat on his skin and pain in his head and nausea in his stomach. He didn't like it at all.

Meg was a mistake. A bad mistake, the kind of mistake that could take a well-ordered life and flip it out of joint. Take his life, for instance. It had been a neat life, a life that was well-ordered without being confining, a life that gave him as much as possible of what he wanted without putting him in a bind. He had spent years in a border town without going on a spree, had had a few drinks every day without letting the stuff take the edge from his self-control. In one night he had thrown that control to the winds. He'd been drunk on tequila, high on marijuana, had gone orgy-nuts in a trap for oversexed tourists. And for what? For a headache, and a sick stomach, and unsteady legs, and a coating of sweat.

So what if she was smart, if she was beautiful, if she spoke her mind and knew what she wanted and went out and got it and was good in bed? Great in bed. So what?

He stood up. His legs were in slightly better shape this time and his stomach was settling down. He opened the door of the stall shower and let the water run. When it was the right temperature he stood under it. For a moment be thought that the spray would knock him over, but it did not, and he let the water wash away some of the grime. He lathered his hard body with bar soap and rinsed more dirt away. He soaped himself a few more times, rinsed a few more times, turned off the shower and dried himself with a towel. He felt cleaner now, but some of the griminess seemed to have lodged itself beneath his skin. As though the filth were a part of him, he thought. As though he'd absorbed it and it was a permanent acquisition.

His mouth had a vile taste to it. He brushed his teeth half a dozen times until the flavor of the toothpaste had driven away some of the unpleasantness. He left the bathroom and put on fresh clean clothes. Meg was still sleeping. He went to her side, gripped her shoulder and shook her roughly. For several seconds she made no response whatsoever. Then she opened her eyes, blinked, closed them. He shook her again, harder. This time her eyes stayed open.

"I'm going away," he told her. "When I leave, get up. You can take a shower if you want. Then get some clothes on and get out of here. Don't come back."

She did not understand.

"It's over," he said. "I don't know just what it was in the first place but it's over. You've still got your twelve hundred, or most of it. Take it and go. I don't want to see you again."

"Why not?"

"I live my own life," he said. "You're not part of it. I live alone and I like it. I want to keep it that way."

She said, "You said you loved me."

"I said that?"

"Last night."

He decided he must have been awfully drunk. "I was wrong," he said. "I don't love anybody. I'm leaving now. Be gone when I get back, Meg. Go to the airport and catch a plane to Chicago."

"I don't want to go to Chicago."

"Somewhere else, then. New York, Los Angeles, Cleveland. I don't care where, but go."

"Can't I even stay in your town?"

Her eyes were bitter. "You shouldn't," he told her. "Paso brings out the worst in you; stay here and you'll fall apart."

"I was all right before I met you."

"That's the point. Get away from me and you'll be all right again. Get away from me and from El Paso."

"You're mad about last night?"

"I'm just sick of it."

"You showed me around," she said. "You took me every place. I don't see why you're angry at me."

"I'm not angry," he said. "I just want to get you out of my sight."

"Damn it—"

"So long," he said. "I'll be gone for three or four hours. You'd better not be here when I come back or I'll throw you out on your butt. You can call a cab and take it to the airport."

"My bags are at the Warwick."

"Then stop at the Warwick and pick them up. So long, Meg."

She didn't answer, which was just as well. He got his wallet, stuffed it into his hip pocket, and left the house. The Olds was in the garage and the key was still in the ignition. Sloppy, he thought. Somebody could have stolen the car. He got behind the wheel, started the car, backed out of the driveway.

He drove to the diner where he'd eaten—when? Yesterday? It seemed more like a month ago. He parked at the curb and went inside. The whole idea of food sent his stomach flipping again, but he knew that passing up a meal would only make everything that much worse. Alcohol knocked you for a loop. It drained your system of vitamins, set you back a few pegs. You had to stuff yourself full of food to get on an even footing again.

He ordered a large glass of tomato juice with a double dash of Worcestershire Sauce. It was supposed to be a hangover recipe. He drank it down, coughed, and ordered eggs sunny side with fried potatoes and toast and coffee. He didn't have ham with his eggs. Meat, just then, would have been too hard to keep down.

After five cups of black coffee, enough to give him a very minor case of caffeine nerves, he got back in the car and drove to the cigar store. There were no customers on the scene when he got there. He asked the clerk if anything was new.

"Your daily double bet ran out," the man said.

He'd completely forgotten making the bet. He handed the man a five dollar bill and told him to play three and five again.

"What else?"

"The feller from Miami Beach," the man said. "He was around again, still looking for someone to give him a game."

"The gin rummy man?"

"The same. Says he's leaving town tomorrow morning, him and his fishtail Cadillac. Wants to find some action before it's time to go."

"He got business in Paso?"

"I'd suppose so. Why else would he be here?"

Marty nodded. "Where's he staying?"

"The Warwick. Only the best, I suspect."

Meg's hotel. "He had some horse bets," Marty said. "How'd he do on those?"

"Poorly. One winner, the rest run out of the money. He lost most of what he bet."

Marty lit a cigarette. He had smoked three of them at the diner. This was the day's fourth, and the first that almost tasted the way it was supposed to. He drew on it, inhaled, let the smoke trickle out slowly.

"You got his name?"

"Name's Simon. Don't know his first name, though."

Marty nodded again. He went to the phone booth, dropped a dime and dialed the Warwick. He asked the desk for Mr. Simon, from Florida. After a few seconds a throaty voice asked him who he was and what he wanted.

"My name is Marty Granger," he said. "A cigar store Indian says you play gin."

"Whattaya know," Simon said. "You play."

"I play."

"He tell you the stakes?"

"He told me and they're fine."

Simon paused. "No insult," he said finally. "If you're a sharp, I'm not interested. I'm from Miami Beach, we play a lotta gin out there, we get a lot of card mechanics. If you're one of them, let's forget it. Because I'll know if you try anything."

"I play straight."

"You better."

"That works both ways."

Simon said, "You don't have to worry. Me, I'm too smart to drink and too old to chase whores. That leaves gambling, and gin's the only game I know. I don't have to cheat. I just want a game."

"Your room?"

"Fine."

"Tonight, after dinner?"

"Fine again."

Marty hung up. The cigar clerk said, "You playing the feller?"

"Yeah."

"I thought you didn't like the game."

"I don't," Marty said. "Listen, I'm going to sit in a Turkish bath for the afternoon, I want to sit and sweat for a while. He's going to drop in here, lay ten or twenty bucks on you for setting things up, then pump you for what you know about me."

"What do I say?"

"The truth. I'm a gambler and my game's poker. I don't play much gin but I figure this is an easy way to make a fast killing. I'm honest. I just think he's a lousy gin player and I can beat him with my eyes closed."

"Is that last part the truth?"

Marty thought about it. "No," he said. "He's probably good enough. But let him think I'm cocky about it. It never hurts."

Lily was drinking a Cuba Libre, sipping it slowly, She was in the bar where she had met Cassie and the others the first time around. Benno was off somewhere. The rest of them were at the table with Lily, drinking rum Cokes of their own.

"How'd it go last night, baby?"

She looked at Paul. He sat with one arm around Didi while his other hand gripped his rum Coke. "It moved," she said. "It was all right."

"You dig the stage bit?"

"I made it."

She looked at Cassie. The girl with red hair had a strange expression in her eyes. She's in love with me, Lily thought. The stupid dyke is in love with me. If I say I just managed the bit on stage her feelings get hurt. I got to be nice to her.

So she said, "It was kind of a gas. But I didn't exactly dig having the whole world tuned in, you know? I didn't know balling was a spectator sport, like."

Cassie beamed. Actually, Lily thought, the reverse was a little closer to the truth. It was better on stage than it was alone with Cassie. When they were on the black-sheeted bed it was just part of an elaborate con, just a balling act to break up the customers and put them on in spades. But when they were alone in the hotel room it was just her and Cassie. It wasn't an act then and she wasn't a performer. She was a dyke's sweetheart, a butch's femme. She couldn't write it off as part of the job. Cassie was gay, and Lily was gay when she slept with Cassie. And, like, who needed it? Not her, not Lily Daniels. Not at all.

"And the tricks?"

"The tricks were a big drag."

"No kicks?"

"No kicks at all," she said. "Where's the kick in balling somebody who's paying for it? No kicks there, man."

That, at least, was the truth. She had had thirteen men, one after the other, in the little room where Ringo put her to work. Somehow she had managed to preserve her cool, had managed to isolate her mind and keep it from tuning itself in on what her body was doing. That was the vital part—retaining your cool, holding on to remoteness.

Twice, the cool had faded. One time she was with a young kid, a boy only a year or two older than herself, a kid without experience or confidence. He had had trouble, had been impotent at first, and she saw his face contort with tears of frustration and embarrassment.

"Cool it," she had told him. "Lie down, relax."

Then her hands roamed his body and her lips had found him and fondled him. He responded, slowly but surely, and when he took her his passion was real and honest and strong. That time her cool had vanished. That time, somehow, the boy was genuine and important, and her mind synchronized itself with the motions of her loins.

She actually cried after he left her.

The other time was the reverse. That time she was reached not by passion but by revulsion, not by empathy but by contempt and disgust. The trick was a drunk with red eyes and a pot belly, a Midwestern banker on a holiday spree. He had her strip, had her parade the room naked, had her come to him on hands and knees. He told her to turn around, then, and he used her as he might have used a young boy, taking her from behind with his soft hands gripping her by the buttocks and his body punishing her, hurting her. She had been used in that manner before, by Frank in San Francisco one night when he wanted her and her period had prevented more relations. It had been unpleasant enough then, and it was worse now.

So her cool vanished again. And she cried again when he left her, cried bitter tears that stained her cheeks.

"It wasn't that bad," she told Paul now. "All I had to do was hang onto my cool."

She lifted her rum Coke and sipped it; the Coke part was flat and the drink sickening sweet. She put her glass down, wishing that somebody would spring for a bottle of tequila. For a moment she considered buying it herself, then decided against it. Damned if she would pay out her own bread for a batch of vultures. To hell with that.

Because she had to save her money. The more money she earned and the more of it she held onto, the sooner she could get the hell away from Ciudad Juarez. It didn't take a hell of a lot of thinking to lead her to the conclusion that she didn't want to spend the rest of her life with Cassie on a stage and putting out for tourists in a back room. It was easy money, but she could live without it.

Hell, she had the shape and the face. In New York, with the

right connections, she could turn one trick a night and make twice the dough. They didn't have wide-open pervert shows in New York, but they had out-of-town buyers getting the soft-soap routine from New York salesmen, and they paid call girls long bread for being handy in bed. There wouldn't be any sex-on-the-stage crud, and there wouldn't be any thirteen cats a night, and, more important, there wouldn't be any Cassie.

But she couldn't make it without dough. She needed plane fare to New York, first of all, and she needed working capital when she hit town. Money for some really decent clothes, and for a good apartment in a good neighborhood. With that kind of a front she wouldn't have any trouble getting started. A grand would do it neatly.

How was she going to save up a grand in Juarez?

At thirty-five or forty bucks a night, it wouldn't be too easy. It would cost her ten a day to stay alive, so she could save, with luck, around a hundred fifty a week. But there would be extra expenses, and there would be four or five days a month when work was biologically out of the question. It would take ten weeks at a minimum, with twenty more like it. That was a hell of a long time to spend in Juarez.

Well, she thought, maybe something would turn up. As things stood, she had a gig which wasn't too horrible. She would save as much bread as she possibly could and wait for her break to come. When it came, she'd grab onto it fast and not let go.

She hoisted her Cuba Libre and drained it.

Meg sat on her bed in the Hotel Warwick and studied the front page of the El Paso evening paper. SEX FIEND TORTURES, KILLS WOMAN, the headline shrieked. She read through the story and shuddered. A woman had been murdered, her breasts and belly and thighs slashed in a few hundred places, her fingers and toes sliced off, her body covered with burns. The paper was explicit, mentioning the toothmarks on the woman's breasts and sex organs. It said, in a masterpiece of understatement, that the murder victim had been criminally attacked.

Now wasn't that something? A bizarre euphemism, she thought. Burn a girl's breasts, slash her to ribbons, shear off her fingers and toes, and you have to give her a medical examination to tell that she's been *criminally attacked*. Say *rape,* for Christ's sake and to hell with euphemisms. The poor girl had been criminally attacked, all right, whether she was raped or not. How criminal could you get?

She tossed the paper away and lit a cigarette. She felt rotten and the cigarette tasted about as good as she felt. Leave El Paso, Marty had told her. Well, to hell with him. She would stay where she goddamn pleased, and to hell with him.

The bastard. He had a hangover, he was disgusted with himself, so she got stuck with the blame for it. What in hell had she done? She'd let go, she'd gotten hotter than hell and higher than heaven, and so she'd released all the tension that had been bound up within her. She didn't blame herself and she didn't blame Marty. As far as she was concerned, blame never entered the picture.

She had a hangover herself, of course, but that didn't mean she felt bad. Alcoholic remorse, or post-alcoholic remorse, struck her as a load of crap. She had made her hangover easier with a double of Beefeater on the rocks instead of sitting around and taking the pledge. And, instead of crying about how whorishly she had acted, she was pretty well pleased with herself. It had been a lot of fun. It was something she would do again, when the mood struck her. The simple fact that she had let herself go sexually was not going to make her run to the nearest doctor for a hysterical hysterectomy. Her mind didn't work that way.

Leave El Paso? To hell with you, Marty Granger. To hell with you, and go screw yourself, and so forth. She would leave El Paso when she was goddamn good and ready. If she felt like it, she'd spend the rest of her life in this rotten town.

Marty Granger. Who was he, anyway? Just a tinhorn gambler, just a punk with a lot of style and not much more. For a while there she had thought maybe she was falling in love with him. Whatever it was, it certainly wasn't love. He was a stylish guy and he was good in bed, but you couldn't take something like that and make a thing called love out of it. And what the hell was love, anyway? A big word that added up to nothing.

She chucked the cigarette in the toilet and lit a fresh one. Love? You could get in trouble confusing a bad case of hot pants with love. What she'd had for Marty had been hot pants. It was what she had now. She was sure as hell not in love.

Hot pants? Yeah, that was what she had, all right. But not, thank God, for Marty Granger.

She stood up and began to pace the room.

It was unnatural, she thought. But what was natural, anyway? She had hot emotions, and she had them for a honey blonde with big breasts. If someone had suggested two days ago that she might want to make love with a girl, she wouldn't even have slapped him. She would have laughed aloud, because the idea would have been so ridiculous that she couldn't so much as take offense.

But now it seemed far less ridiculous. Last night she had watched a redhead and a blonde make love, and watching the two of them had been the most exciting experience of her life. Before that, a picture of two lesbians going at it was the most arousing picture in a folder of filth. And last night, after the show, she had watched Marty and a Mexican tramp having a go at it, and watching had made her hot. But she hadn't been hot for Marty. She'd been itching to fill her own hands with the Mex girl's breasts, had itched to get down on her knees and kiss the little slut.

That blonde, she thought. That big-boobed blonde. Now wouldn't that be something? God in heaven!

What the hell, she thought. She was in El Paso, and a Mexican hot spot was just a few hundred yards away across an artificial border. Get out of El Paso? Not on your life, Marty Granger. She could cross that imaginary border, and she could find out just what it was like to have a lesbian fling. It wasn't as though it would turn her into a dyke or anything, it would just be an experiment.

A little excitement. That was all she needed—just a little excitement. A little stacked-blonde excitement, to be precise.

She laughed, wondering what it would be like. She tried to imagine herself walking into Delia's Place and asking the head-waiter to fix her up with the blonde. He'd probably sell tickets.

What would he do, for God's sake? What would he say? Well, she would find out soon enough.

They had his picture on the front page. It was a two-column cut about four inches square and it wasn't a good likeness at all, the same picture they had run in the Tulsa papers. But he was glad to see any picture at all. The early editions hadn't even had his name let alone his picture. And here it was, right smack dab in the middle of the front page.

He read the article all the way through. Outside of the iden-tification, it didn't have much that was new. The police were working, it said, on a wide variety of clues. He felt like laughing aloud. Clues? He had spelled it out for them by leaving bloody fingerprints on the wall over Audrey's bed. What more did they need in the way of clues? They knew everything they had to know. Everything but where he was, and they'd have to work some to find that out.

Of course, he thought, it was only a matter of time. They would block roads, would throw a cordon around El Paso and

Juarez, and gradually they would draw the net tighter until they had him in it. Any day they would check the hotel he was in right now, and when they did they would have him. No sense sitting around waiting to be captured. No time.

That night he had placed his razor under the mattress. Now he took it out and opened it, rubbing his thumb across the blade. It was duller than it had been when he had bought it. The blade had done hard work cutting through the bones of Audrey's toes and fingers. Naturally it had lost a certain amount of its keenness. Maybe he should have bought the leather strop after all.

He got to his feet, put his clothes on again. It was dinner time and he was hungry. He wondered if they would recognize him outside from the photo in the papers. He guessed that they wouldn't. The picture showed him with a prison brushcut and he didn't look like that at all. Besides, if he stayed in his room all the time he would die slowly of starvation.

Outside he found a chili joint and had a howl of hot chili with cheese and a cup of soup. The razor was not under his mattress now. It was in his pocket, ready for action.

Because, he thought, it was time. Killing time. He left the chili joint and began walking around the city. It was early and the sky was light, but he had learned something the night before, had gained a valuable lesson during the wonderful time he had spent with Audrey. The lesson was this—you did not need the cloak of darkness, did not need silent and unlighted streets. You needed only privacy.

He knew where to find privacy. You walked until you found a certain type of street, and then everyone was all too happy to offer you privacy. From there on, it was easy.

When he had walked for half an hour he found the area he was searching for. Crib Row, the cheap-whore section of town. There were row upon row of one-room shanties, each painted the same drab gray, and each with a woman in front seated upon either a cane chair or an upended orange crate. They shouldn't have started that early in the evening, he thought. In the light, they were too ugly. They should wait until darkness.

But it didn't matter.

He walked along a crib-lined street, waiting. A woman clutched at his arm, her dull eyes bright with promise. She told him in poor English just what she would do for him.

She was too old, and pregnant as well. He kept walking.

"Frenchie, Joe?"

Last night he had been Mac; today, he was Joe. The girl who offered herself was younger than the rest, maybe twenty-five, maybe even less. Her face was not pretty at all and her chest was flat, which explained what she was doing on Crib Row. But she was young.

"Frenchie," she said eagerly, earnestly. "Ony a dollar, Joe. You wanna hot frenchie?"

So his name was Joe, for a while. He put his hand in his pocket. Misreading the gesture, she reached forward and patted him with her fingers. His hand found the razor and held it.

"Let's go," he said. She stood up and he followed her into the shack and closed the door.

CHAPTER EIGHT

Simon was a big man, red in the face, thick in the middle. His hands were pudgy. A few of the blood vessels in his nose were broken, suggestive of high blood pressure rather than alcoholism. He stuck out a hand and Marty shook it. A dead-fish handshake, Marty thought. The kind that made you want to go and wash your hands.

"You're Granger," he said. "Right?"

"Right."

"I got a pair of decks here. Bicycle brand, unopened. Good enough for you?"

"Fine."

"What do they call you? Marty?"

"That's it."

"Have a drink, Marty? Room service sent me up a bottle of Chivas and a pail of ice. Join me?"

"Not just yet."

They sat down in folding chairs on opposite sides of a small card table, evidently also provided by room service. Marty watched as Simon broke open a deck and shuffled it. He riffled the cards elaborately. All right, Marty thought. So you've seen a deck before. I'm duly impressed.

"Marty? Not to offend you, but when I play with a stranger I like to see some front money. You understand?"

"You want to be able to collect when you win. It makes sense."

He took out his wallet and spread bills on the table. There

were a lot of them. Simon smiled graciously and waved a pudgy hand at the bills. Marty stuffed them back in his wallet.

"Now if you want the same privilege—"

"Forget it," Marty told him. "You're driving a Cad, the way I hear it. A Cad is worth more than either of us is going to win or lose."

Simon was still shuffling the cards. "The game is Hollywood," he said. "Spades double, twenty for gin, ten for undercutting. Hundred and fifty points makes a game, ten points a box, a hundred for game. A dollar a point."

"That's a big game."

"Too big?"

"I didn't say that."

Simon put the pack on the table. "Cut for deal," he said. They cut. Marty drew an eight of hearts, while Simon cut to the jack of diamonds.

"Deal," Marty said.

Weaver was strangely calm now. He was in the shanty with the young prostitute, and his hand was in his pocket, holding onto the razor. The shanty was a mess, underclothing heaped in a corner of the little room. The place stank.

Again, he thought, he was doing a favor for a girl. This Mexican whore had less of a life than Audrey. She sold herself for a dollar, sat in front of her filthy crib begging men to make a tramp out of her. Death would probably be a pleasure for her. The poor thing had nothing to lose.

"Frenchie," she said.

He decided that she didn't know much English. She had a feeble-minded look about her. He told her to take off her clothes and she stared at him. He made motions to go with the words, pulling vaguely at his own clothing and then pointing to her. She got the idea and smiled hugely at him. Her teeth, he saw, were worse than his own. Yellow and decayed. It made him a little sick to look at her teeth.

She began to undress and he studied her body dispassionately. Small breasts, still fresh with youth but not much to look at. Thin, bony legs. Hips almost boyish. She was somehow sad when fully dressed, but she was far more pathetic with no clothes on. Poor creature, he told himself. Death would release her from her chains.

"Frenchie," she said again. "A dollar, Joe."

He gave her a dollar. She crumpled it into a paper ball and kept it in her hand, while her other hand went to his clothing. She sat down now, on the edge of the bed, and he stood in front of her. Her one hand still held tight to the crumpled dollar while her other hand made itself busy.

Her hand did not excite him. It was weird now, he thought. There was very little excitement connected with the whole affair. He was going to have sex with this girl, and he was going to kill her, and yet the primary motivation was not overtly sexual. He had not sought out this woman because of any great physical need. He had been sexually satisfied, not excited or keyed-up at all.

Something was different. This same sort of calm, to a lesser degree, had been present when he had first taken Audrey to her room. It was more secure within him now. He had a duty to perform, and the duty was Death. This was his job, his role which he had to play. His enjoyment of the task was secondary at best.

The girl was still handling him. Now she raised her eyes to meet his. She smiled, briefly. Then her mouth opened, and closed.

The caress was one that Weaver had never received before. He let himself relax, let enjoyment wash over him. His hand moved from his pocket, still holding the razor. The girl did not notice it. He flipped it open with a flick of his wrist, and still she did not notice it.

She *did* notice it, however, when he was holding it against her throat.

Her eyes came up again, and this time they rolled in terror. She tried to move her head away, move it from the razor, but his other hand was at the back of her neck and she was unable to move her head at all.

"Keep going," he said gently. "Don't stop."

She went on with what she had been doing but her eyes were on Weaver's face. Now he was doubly excited; the caress, combined with the look of abject terror in the poor girl's eyes, was too much to bear. Desire welled up within him and his brain swam in lust.

"Keep going," he said to her, again. "Keep going, whore, slut, tramp. Keep going."

She probably did not understand the words. But she did understand what was expected of her. She followed his orders while he held the edge of the razor at her tender throat.

He watched her. He saw the horror in her eyes. He looked down past them and saw her poor little breasts. A day ago he would have slashed at those breasts, would have cut them to ribbons until blood dripped from them. But now he was able to restrain himself. Such extra touches were unnecessary, extraneous—just wrapping paper on the main theme. He would not hurt this girl, would not mutilate her.

No.

She caressed him and his passion mounted. He reached the peak in a short amount of time. And, at the precise moment, he struck quickly with the razor, slashing neatly through the girl's throat.

She died quickly, almost instantly. He watched her death

throes with interest then dressed himself. He stopped for a moment to dip his fingers into her blood and leave fingerprints on the wall of the shanty. There was a small water pot in one corner and he used the water in it to wash the blood from the tips of his fingers.

Then, anonymous as the customer of any inexpensive prostitute, he left her shack and closed the door after him.

He was two blocks away before he heard the shrill screams of the girl who had discovered his victim. He walked on without even quickening his pace and an automatic smile spread across his face. His hand touched his pocket, noting with approval that the razor was still there. He kept smiling and kept walking.

Marty picked up his cards, fanned them, arranged them. He glanced quickly at the score pad and saw he was a little over a hundred dollars down. Nothing much at a dollar a point. Hell, they were just getting started. If the final count didn't run a thou one way or the other, it would be a hell of a tight evening.

They had been playing for half an hour, and Marty was beginning to get a line on Simon's game. Simon wasn't a bad player. Marty would have been surprised if he had been; bad players can't play dollar-a-point gin very long without running out of money. Simon played a tight game. He knew the mathematics of the game and he had a good card memory. Those were the two main ingredients.

But Marty was confident. Simon may have been a gin player, he thought, but he himself was a gambler. When card ability was even, you had to play the man along with the cards. You had to case his game and find a way to throw him off stride. This was half of poker, where the cards didn't mean as much as what you could do with them. But it was also part of gin, if only a small part. It was enough to make a difference.

Simon liked to lie back and wait for gin. With the gin bonus twenty-five points and the box bonus only ten points, it wasn't a bad notion. But there was a way to knock it askew. A few fast knocks would get Simon worried. Then, with the right timing, he could get undercut a few times. And by then he'd start to wobble on the ropes.

Marty knocked early, won the hand and picked up all of five points. He got down quick the next hand for fifteen points. The next hand he did the same thing, getting just two points that time.

Simon came back the next hand, or tried to. He knocked with three, and Marty was sitting pretty on two points for an undercut.

"You play a funny game," Simon said.

"I don't play too much gin. My game is poker."

"I never liked it."

Marty riffled the cards. He dealt, turned up the twenty-first card. It was the five of spades.

"This hand's double," he said. He picked up his hand, fanned it, and concentrated on the game.

Meg had dinner at Giardi's, the Italian restaurant where she had eaten her first day in El Paso. She sat alone at a small table at the rear and ordered scampi fra diavolo with a bottle of the best chianti. The shrimps were delicious and the spaghetti was fine. She ate a full meal, drank the whole bottle of sour wine, and left the waiter a good tip. When she went outside the air was far cooler. The rain had stopped shortly after Marty awakened her, and the afternoon had been warm, but now it was fine, not too cool and not too hot.

She took Marty's advice, in part. She left Giardi's and got out of El Paso. She went across the border, to Juarez. In a small cafe near the plaza she ordered tequila and ignored the stares of the cafe's other customers. She drank her tequila and tried to think straight.

As well as she could remember, the lesbian act at Delia's Place had started around ten at night. It was hard to determine how long the act lasted, since it wasn't the sort of thing you could watch while paying attention to the time. But she guessed that it lasted somewhere between fifteen minutes and a half hour. Maybe closer to half an hour, since they made quite a production out of the number.

So she figured on the blonde being ready for action around ten-thirty. She didn't want to watch the floor show again; it would be a little too much, seeing it two nights in a row. She wasn't interested in watching, anyway. She was interested in getting into the act.

In a way, it was less than ridiculous. She was a normal, healthy American woman who, up until a very short time ago, had been married to a rich man in Chicago. But she had since come a long ways from Borden Rector. The four years of sexual and emotional stagnation had made a different woman out of her. Everything had been repressed, bottled up, and now everything was exploding now that someone had taken the cork out.

Where had it started, exactly? There were a dozen answers to that one, but the most logical was the simplest. It had started the minute the divorce decree had come through. Once she was legally free of Borden Rector, once she was no longer his wife and no longer a married woman at all, she was able to let herself go. All the rest had been inevitable.

If she had not bought the pictures in Juarez, she would have been excited elsewhere, by something else. A movie or a magazine would have done what the pictures did. And if she had not been picked up by Marty Granger, some other man would have found her and would have taken her to bed. The floor show at Delia's Place took the top off a lot of things, but some other stimulant would have had the same effect upon her sooner or later. The blonde—the little girl with chunky breasts and a schoolgirl face—was the final object of desire. But the instincts had been there all the time, and would sooner or later have come to the surface, no matter where Meg went or what she did.

She sipped her tequila, lit a cigarette. A man at the bar, a very thin Mexican, was looking her up and down and smiling seductively. There was something very sexy about him but at the moment she was not interested. She wished he would look somewhere else.

Instead, he approached her table. In mildly accented English he asked if he might sit with her.

"I'm waiting for a friend," she said.

"May I wait with you?"

"I'd rather wait alone."

He took the hint and walked sadly back to the bar. She sipped more tequila. Maybe she should have let him sit down, she thought. Maybe she didn't want the blonde after all. Maybe the lesbian bit was just a reaction to the way Marty had acted that morning, just a plate of forbidden fruit with a sign on it that said Eat Me.

There was a way to find out. All she had to do was find another man and let him take her to a bed. Afterward, she would know whether or not she wanted the blonde. Maybe the man would erase any lesbian desires that she had. If that was the case, it would be pointless to find the blonde. She could stick to men.

She did nothing about it, because she didn't have to. She finished a cigarette and started another, and as she was finishing that one the Mexican came once again to her table, a hopeful light in his eyes. He rested his hands on the top of the table and leaned over.

"Your friend has not arrived," he said.

She leaned forward, too, letting him look down the front of her dress. She could feel his eyes burning the tops of her breasts and this excited her. It seemed to excite him as well. His eyes were gleaming.

"May I join you, now?"

"No."

"No?"

"No," she said again, getting to her feet. "No, I'm bored with this bar. Have you a place where we can go?"

He smiled broadly now and took her arm.

Cassie said, "I can hardly wait, Lily. I mean, to do it again tonight. I get a bang out of it. You know what I mean?"

"Sure," Lily said.

"I can't wait at all, is what it is. I want some now, Lily. Before we go over to Delia's."

"Not now."

"Please, baby?"

Lily gritted her teeth. This was a real pain in the rear, she thought. The redheaded flat-chested little dyke never let her alone. At least with a man you got a little rest. A man could only keep it up so long and then he let you have a moment's peace. But Cassie couldn't stop itching. A gay nympho, Lily thought. She's got to be getting it every other minute or she shivers and starts to fold.

"No," she said.

"Just a little taste, Lily. Just let me rub up against you a little bit, or something. God, I'm flipping!"

"So flip, then."

"Lily—"

"I think I know why Didi left you, Cass. You never let the poor chick alone. Get off my back, huh?"

"Aw, Lily—"

It was too much to take. She had to get the hell away from Cassie before she went nuts. The work was a drag, but the work was only a few hours a day, and Cassie looked as though she was going to become a full-time proposition. She had to get out of Juarez, had to go back to the States and set herself up the right way.

But it came back to the same thing every time. To do that, she needed money. A thou, say. And how in hell was she going to get her hands on a thousand dollars?

"Please, Lily. Like I want it so bad I can taste it."

"So taste it. But don't taste me."

"I'll go nuts, Lily. I'll go out of my head!"

She stood up and walked to the door. She yanked it open, then turned for a parting look at Cassie. The redhead was on the bed, her scrawny hips rolling involuntarily.

"Use a damn candle," she said. "I'll see you at Delia's. At ten. Then we'll do whatever you want."

"Gin," Marty said.

"Again?"

"Again."

"Nuts," Simon said.

❀

The Mexican had a lot of money. Unlike Marty, he didn't live in a house. He had an apartment in the better section of Juarez, in a building with a doorman and a self-service elevator. His apartment was tastefully furnished and his bed had smooth sheets.

In the bedroom, they did not talk. Meg got out of her dress, brushed her long dark hair over her shoulders. The Mexican removed all his clothes and came over to her. He took her into his arms and his mouth found hers. He had a thin mustache, and it tickled her when he kissed her. She almost laughed, but then his arms were tight around her like steel bands and she did not want to laugh at all. She felt her breasts being crushed against his chest and passion leaped to life within her body.

He removed her bra and took her breasts in his hands. He stroked them and pinched her nipples and her breath came quicker and harder. He lifted her in strong arms, carried her to the bed.

She lay on her back and he began to touch her. His hands were surprisingly gentle for such a strong man. He fondled her breasts, rubbed her stomach, stroked the softness of her thighs. She felt the heat spread from the places where his fingers touched her until her whole body was a sheet of liquid flame. She moaned softly and his mouth came down upon hers, his tongue stabbing into her mouth and finding her tongue. She wrapped her arms about his body, holding him close, feeling the heat of him matching her own heat. Her legs drew him in close.

Until then her mind had been working frenetically. She had thought of Borden Rector, of Marty, of the blonde. But now all thoughts gave way to reality. She was with this man, this Mexican, and nothing else was at all relevant for the time being. She was on his bed in his bedroom, and he was upon her, ready to take her. Nothing else mattered at all except what he and she were about to do.

His hard-muscled chest against her breasts—that was real, that had meaning. Her nipples were suffused with desire and the pressure of his body against them was making her wild with lust. His body against her body—that, too, was real and meaningful. She wriggled her hips and her body shivered at the electric charge that seared through her.

He kissed her again, then moved away from her to kiss first one breast and then the other. And then his lips darted away to plant a kiss high on her thigh. A tingling kiss, a chilling feverish kiss. This was real.

And it was still more real when he threw himself once more upon her. His firmness searched for her, stabbed for her, found her. She groaned with pain and pleasure as he forced his way into her, and then all the pain was nothing compared with the pleasure as their bodies moved together, strained together—

She gripped his buttocks with her hands and clawed him with her fingernails. She raked his back with her nails, drawing blood. He thrust himself into her, again and again and again, until she was screaming out her raw lust at the top of her lungs.

Their fulfillments were simultaneous, and complete. He lay in her arms for several minutes, inert and half-dead. Then he rolled free of her embrace and instantly fell asleep.

But she did not sleep. Instead she got up from his bed, put on her clothing, left his apartment and walked on the streets outside. She had had a man, a man who had loved her magnificently. She had had him, and her body still was warm and glowing from his lovemaking, still tingling from his embrace.

And she still wanted the blonde at Delia's Place.

*

Marty shuffled the cards. He was ahead now, nicely ahead. He was into Simon for over a thousand dollars and it looked as though he had the Miami Beach gin player on the run. Simon knew his game but he was rocky now. And he was getting too much of a glow from the Chivas. The Scotch was getting to him. He was starting to do dumb things, picking up the wrong cards on speculation, throwing Marty his card because his memory was slipping, generally easing up on his game.

Like fish in a barrel, Marty thought. He put the pack on the table and Simon cut the cards. He took up the pack again and began dealing. There might be easier ways to make a quick killing, he thought. But it would be hard to name three.

Or even one.

He watched Simon pick up his cards and spread them. Simon's lips curled downward.

"Lousy hand," he said. "All I get is lousy hands."

"Cards'll do that."

"They've been running bad, Granger. Ready for a drink now?"

He couldn't turn the man down forever. "Sure," he said. "But make it a short one, huh?"

Simon filled two water tumblers with Chivas Regal, added an ice cube to each. Some of the Scotch spilled on the table top. Marty took a small sip. It was good Scotch.

It was a fine way to pass an evening, he thought. Good Scotch and good cards, and he'd leave the room with more money than he'd had in his pocket walking in. It was enough to chase away any thoughts he might otherwise have had about the woman he'd thrown out of his bed this morning. The one who at this very moment was probably on a plane heading north—if she'd followed his instructions. Or who, if she hadn't, might still be in her room in this very hotel, perhaps even on this floor. Maybe lying naked in bed or lounging in a warm bath. For sure as beautiful and exciting and electric as he remembered. Not that he'd spent the day thinking about her. She hadn't come to mind more than eight or nine times. At most ten. He'd suspected she might, and it was part of the reason he'd finally agreed to this session, even though gin wasn't his game—so he wouldn't spend the night sitting alone and thinking and maybe regretting his decision. There was no place for regret in a gambler's mind. You played your hand or you folded it and you moved on, and you didn't look back to see what cards you might have drawn.

Marty took another sip of the Scotch.

Simon picked up a card, fitted it into his hand, discarded. Marty picked up his discard and filled a run with it. He discarded.

Five minutes later Marty dropped a card face down.

"Knocking?"

"Uh-huh."

"How many?"

"Two."

"Nuts," Simon said.

When the spotlight died, Lily got the hell off the stage. Ringo patted her gingerly on the rump as she scurried past him. "Good show, kid," he told her. "They loved you."

She hurried to her room, soaked a towel under the water faucet and began sponging off her body. Cassie had been impossible, and she didn't care whether their little act had been good or bad. It was an everloving pain in the neck, a drag from start to finish.

She felt filthy all over now. Cassie hadn't been acting on the stage, not in the least. The redhead had been hotter than a Franklin stove and the fact that Lily wasn't at all interested didn't have much to do with it one way or the other. When they were on the stage, Lily had to play Cassie's game. Whether she wanted to or not.

Well, it wouldn't last much longer. She couldn't stay in a dead-end town like this or she would go off her nut. She had to get out.

She went to work, cleaning herself off. It was waste of time, though; as soon as she got halfway clean there would be a man at the door, and from that point on she wouldn't get a hell of a lot of rest. Then, when she was done for the night, Cassie would expect her to go to bed with her. Well, Cassie had another guess coming, dammit. She'd find another hotel and take a room of her own. She'd rather pay a buck or two a day than have to fight off a redhead lezzie twenty-four hours a day, seven days a week.

There was a knock on the door.

She sighed, got into a wrapper and went to the door. Pancho was standing there, an American tourist at his side. Pancho stepped out of the way and the American walked into the room. He had already paid the money, of course. They paid in advance, giving their money to Ringo, and then Pancho took them around. She never saw the money. According to Pancho, some of them tipped the girls. But she hadn't gotten any tips the night before and she was beginning to think it was a load of crap.

"Saw you on stage," the American said. "You looked like you were havin' one old hell of a time."

Lily said. "No speak English."

"Huh? You kiddin' me?"

"No speak English."

"You ain't a Mex, sister."

"Portuguese," she said, faking what she hoped was a Portuguese accent. It was bad enough having to sleep with the bastards, she thought, but she wasn't going to talk to them, too. Balling was one thing. Companionship was another, and she wasn't getting paid for it.

The American was in a hurry, anyway. She got out of her wrapper, then helped him undress. He pawed her body with his sweaty hands while she tried to pretend she was getting excited. He called her dirty names, evidently thinking she couldn't understand him, and she struggled not to get annoyed by the things he said to her.

At least he only wanted to make love in a conventional manner. He had a slight variation, in that he wanted her to do all the work. He lay on his back, she straddling him. They made love in that position, the man smiling up at her and speaking to her in American gutter-slang. When it was over he dressed and left. She did not even bother to wash herself off. Then she put on the wrapper and waited for the next one.

A pair of kids came next, New York college boys having a summer sleighride in Mexico. They took turns with her, one watching while the other made love to her. They were young, and their experience had evidently been limited to the back seats of cars, so they weren't much of a problem. They had no staying power and little imagination. In a very short time they were on their way and she was once again waiting for another trick to make the scene.

No sooner had she re-wrapped herself in her wrapper than there was another knock at the door. She went to it and threw it open. Pancho was standing there, a fantastic expression on his usually expressionless face.

She saw why.

At Pancho's side, instead of the usual man, was a woman.

The woman had long black hair, and her face was beautiful.

Now she pressed a coin into Pancho's palm and pushed past him into Lily's room. Her eyes were shining. She turned to close the door, then moved toward Lily.

"Hello," she said. "My name is Meg Rector. You're very lovely, dear."

Oh, Christ! Lily thought.

She's lovely! Meg thought.

Meg's knees were turning to water. She could feel the dizzy wave sweep over her body, dissolving the bones of her hips. She seemed to be unable to keep her balance except by parting her knees.

She had to do it in a quick spasm of motion, or she would have fallen.

The blonde was staring at her.

"My God, you got it bad, don't you?"

"Oh!—Oh, I—I can't…" It was like trying to move underwater, caught in a terrible tide. She reached for the blonde girl; if she didn't reach the blonde girl, she would give way instantly and be swept down and away, writhing and jerking helplessly in the lonely dark.

"I—I can't wait!" Meg gasped out.

The blonde girl shrugged her shoulders. The wrapper slithered down her golden body, revealing her breasts, then her belly, and then the full, round thighs that met breathtakingly at her hips.

"Oh!" Meg cried. "I—I want my clothes off, too! I want—"

"Sure, honey," the blonde said, moving forward. "I know what you want. The bed's over here." She began unfastening Meg's dress.

❖

I've got to figure some way of getting out of this place, Lily thought tiredly as she stripped the quivering brunette and led her—shoved her, was more like it—over onto the bed. The brunette's hands were all over her. *I can't take much more of this!*

But Lily was a pro, and all the time she did these things, she kept smiling.

CHAPTER NINE

He looked into the cracked mirror and smiled at the image of his own ugliness. There had been a girl in Tulsa, and the cops found her in an alley with her flesh chewed and her head beaten to pulp. There had been a woman in El Paso, and the cops found her in her own room with her toes and fingers chopped off and her body cut to ribbons. Now there was a girl in Juarez, a prostitute, and the cops would find her nude and dead, with her throat neatly slashed.

Maybe he wanted to get caught. Or maybe, knowing that capture was inevitable, he wanted to fit all sensations into the time that remained to him. But now he could not sleep. He was alone and at peace, but he could not sleep and he could not remain in his hotel room. He couldn't even stay in Juarez. There was a voice now, a shrill voice screaming inside his skull, urging him to go to El Paso. The voice did not merely urge. It commanded. He had to cross the border once again. He had to take the chance of capture so that he could strike again in El Paso, his razor finding another victim.

It would be simple to cross the border, he told himself. It had been simple enough the first time, coming into Juarez from Texas. Of course, they had not had his picture then, had not been on the lookout for a man answering his description. But the picture was a poor one. Besides, he had killed in El Paso. The border patrol would hardly expect him to sneak *into* El Paso, from Mexico.

All he had to do was be calm and nonchalant about it. He remembered a picture, an old movie set somewhere in Eastern

Europe, where the entire area was up in arms because a were-wolf was on the loose. He remembered how the werewolf, in human form, had gone so far as to join in the hunt parties, biding his time in the fields and forests until the hunt party had broken apart and he was alone with a girl.

Weaver smiled, remembering. The man had turned into a wolf then, his teeth growing into fangs, his fingernails turning to claws. And then he sprang upon the girl, his jaws going for her throat, his claws raking her breasts. The girl would scream, and the girl would die.

In the end, he remembered, they pierced the werewolf's heart with a huge wooden stake. He would never forget the sound the werewolf made. A long, tremulous shriek. Horrible.

He pushed the memories from his mind, combed his black hair once more over his low forehead, and left his room. He walked easily, calmly, in the street outside. He mingled with crowds, thick as flies in the late summer night. He headed, slowly but very surely, toward the border.

It would be easy, he thought. Very easy. And it would strike terror into their hearts. One day a victim in El Paso, the next day a pair of victims, one on each side of the border.

Still, though, he could not entirely rid his mind of the death-scream of the werewolf. Horrible, very horrible.

Meg lay on her back on the bed. Lily was kissing her now, kissing her lips, penetrating her mouth with her warm smooth tongue. Meg opened her eyes and looked at the blonde's perfect body. This isn't wrong, she thought. Wanting someone like this cannot be wrong. This is normal, and beautiful.

Her hands moved now, settling on Lily's shoulders and caressing them. She pulled slightly and Lily's body lowered itself so that the girl's firm breasts rubbed Meg's own. Meg's nipples were taut with desire. She sighed and her arms tightened around Lily.

Lily slipped away, her lips flicking out to catch Meg's breast. Meg tightened the muscles in her legs, stretched out her arms, letting her passion whirl her around and wrap her up. Now the girl was kissing one nipple and rolling the other between the fingers of her left hand, while petting Meg further down with her right hand.

It was maddening, electrifying. It was enough to drive a person wild. It was time and space on fire, exploding.

"Honey—"

"What?"

"You want me to do it now?"

Her heart stopped. "B...b-b-both of us," she managed finally.

"Huh?"

"I mean both."

The blonde was laughing. Don't laugh, Meg thought fiercely. Don't laugh, my Lily, my baby, my darling. I don't want this to be funny and I don't want it to be cheap. I want it to be perfect.

"You're the boss," Lily was saying. "You're calling the shots, sister. I won't argue with you."

"Don't you like it?"

"Sure, I like it."

"Then—"

She was not called upon to finish the sentence. Lily started to work on her once again, teaching her things she had never known about before, bringing life to areas of her body which bad never previously tingled with desire. She remembered Marty, and the nameless Mexican, and just as quickly she forgot them both. They were nothing. They had never mattered at all. This was the real thing, the only thing she had ever really wanted from the beginning. This was Life.

Lily showed her how to lie down on the bed. She followed Lily's instructions, lying on her side with her legs hanging over the foot of the bed. Lily lay opposite her, and their faces were together. She looked upside down into Lily's eyes. Lily moved further down and their mouths met. She had never kissed anyone upside down before. It turned out to be completely workable, and quite nice.

Lily moved again. Now the blonde girl's lovely neck was near Meg's lips. She rained kisses upon Lily's neck, letting her lips glide over the very smooth skin. Lily was doing the same for her.

Lily moved, again. And now Meg took Lily's breasts in her hands and brought them to her lips. She kissed Lily's breasts while the blonde was giving her the same treatment. What a wonderful idea, she thought. Kiss and be kissed. You had to be upside down to do it, but it was worth the effort. It felt divine.

She nipped at Lily's nipples with hungry teeth. Lily's skin was soft and her nipples were firm little red jewels in the pinkness of her breasts. Meg shivered with delight.

When Lily moved again, they kissed each other's stomachs. Meg pressed her face to the blonde's firm belly and cupped Lily's buttocks with her hands. She rubbed the girl, kissed her.

Lily moved again.

This time, Meg thought, it was for real. This time it was all the way, no holds barred, nothing held in reserve. The fact that she was a prostitute's customer and that Lily was performing a service had nothing to do with anything. This was *real*—

Very real, terribly real. Her body turned over with brand new sensations and spilled over with fearful lust. She gave as good as she got, making Lily scream happily with passion. This wasn't faking, she told herself. This was real. Lily was alive, on fire, responding magnificently to the caresses Meg was giving her.

It lasted for a very long time. It was not at all like with a male, Meg discovered. There was no tremendous build-up, no speedy climb to a sharp peak. Here the rise was gradual, the ascent a gentle one. The pleasure grew more and more intense, and, when Nirvana was within sight, the road flattened out and lasted for half of eternity.

Then, at last, it was over. Meg shifted position on the bed and let her eyes close. She was whole and complete now, fulfilled as she had never been before. Her whole body glowed with the phenomenal delights which Lily had shown her.

Marty said, "I leave at four."

"Four?"

"That's the idea."

Simon had an unhappy expression on his face. "I don't like it," he said. "I thought this was going to be a long game. Four, now—that isn't much at all."

"That's five hours from now."

Simon chewed a pencil. "I make it that I'm behind another five yards on the three games we just finished. That's a little better than three gees so far, Marty."

"A little better."

"A bad run of cards."

"Not that bad," Marty said. "The stakes are big and it's a loose game. I haven't beaten you that bad. No blitzes yet."

"There's time." Simon smiled thinly. "You don't beat me so bad. You beat me consistent."

"That's because I play better gin."

Simon looked angry. "You think so?"

"I know so. Look at the score if you don't agree. It says I'm three grand better than you already."

"Look, you son of a—"

Marty smiled. This, he thought, was what he liked. He could feel no pity for Simon. The man had more money than he needed, so he chose to play stupid cards for stakes that were too high. He got rattled easily and he drank too freely. Well, he was paying for it. It would be easy to let him off the hook, to throw the edge his way and hold the loss to a thousand dollars or two. But Marty didn't want that.

Meg had brought out the cruelty in him. He did not simply want to win a few thousand from Simon. He wanted to walk out of the Warwick at four in the morning with everything Simon had, every cent, plus the Cadillac, plus Simon's watch and ring. He wanted to make the fat bastard crawl. He wanted to ruin the louse.

"Shuffle 'em good, Granger."

"Don't worry," Marty said. "I don't have to cheat."

"You don't think I play worth a damn?"

"That's the idea."

"You're cocky, Granger."

Marty let himself smile again. That was the way, he thought. Get the bastard mad. You didn't play well when you were mad. You made it a personal contest and you fought the cards, and whatever game you were playing you blew it all to hell. It worked that way in poker and it worked that way in gin. You couldn't play well when you were mad.

You could play hating. That never hurt. You could hate a man with a clear cool hate and only triple your efficiency. Hating Simon didn't hurt anything. It let him play coolly, let him close in for the kill without giving a damn how much he hurt Simon.

"You sure of yourself, Granger?"

"You could call it that."

"Hell, maybe the game's too cheap for you. Want to up the ante a little?"

"I still leave at four."

"Four, schmore. Two bucks a point?"

"Fine." It would be five in an hour, he thought. And then Simon would start to turn green.

Lily said, "Let me get this straight. You want *what*?"

"I want you."

"But—"

"I want to leave this city, and I want you to come with me. That's all there is to it."

"Yeah, but why?"

Lily watched the dark-haired woman. She was chewing on her lower lip now and her eyes were downcast. "I don't know why," she said. "I divorced my husband a week ago. He gave me a lot of money. And last night I won twelve hundred dollars at the roulette wheel. I thought maybe you could help me spend some of the money."

That wouldn't be hard to take, Lily thought. That would be a kind of a groove. It would get her the hell out of Juarez and it would put a lot of miles between her and Cassie.

"Where would we go?"

"I don't know," Meg said, "New York, perhaps."

"I could dig that. You a dyke?"

"Perhaps. You're the first girl I've ever made love to."

"Yeah?"

"Yes."

Twelve hundred bills, Lily thought. Plus a hell of a lot more from her old man. All she had to do was string this Meg broad for a while and she'd hit pay dirt. She'd be out of Juarez and into New York, and from there on it was her ball game. She could milk Meg for a stake big enough to set herself up. Whatever happened after that was anybody's guess.

"Listen," she said, "why me?"

"Because I want you."

"What do we do, then? Just split out of here and head for New York?"

"You could spend the night with me at my hotel," Meg said. "The Warwick, in El Paso. And we could get a morning jet to New York. We'd buy clothes and see plays and eat at good restaurants."

"And make it."

"And make love. That's right."

That was her little part of the bargain, Lily thought. Wherever she went, that was her part of the bargain. Whether it was a ride to El Paso or a job at a whorehouse or a trip to New York, she paid with the only legal tender she had, her own hot little body. Well, what was wrong with that? Meg didn't want anything more than the rest of the world wanted. And Meg offered a better price for it.

She said, "It's a deal."

"Can we go now? Back to the hotel, I mean."

Lily thought quickly. This still could turn out to be some kind of a con, she realized. Meg could spend a night with her in the rack and then change her mind on the whole deal. It was worth taking the chance, but it wasn't worth kicking over her job. If she went now and the deal with Meg fell through, Ringo might not take her back.

"I'd better stick around here, like," she said. "Until closing, I mean. I got to finish the evening."

Meg looked disappointed.

"Only until three-thirty or four," she added. "That's just a few hours. You could sit out front and wait for me. Have a few drinks and watch the show."

"I don't want to see the show. I saw it last night."

"There's a bar across the street. A quiet place. You could take a seat there and cool it while I finish up. Then I could like meet you as soon as I get out of this joint and we could make it across the border."

"All right."

Meg stood up. She was fully dressed now, and she looked coolly remote, with none of lust's after-effects showing. Lily studied her. She was still a little suspicious.

"Meg?"

"What, dear?"

"I want to know your angle, Meg. What's in it for you?"

"Sex."

Lily smiled. "Solid. You aren't on a love kick, are you?"

"No."

"Because if you're in love with me or something—"

"I'm not," Meg said. "I don't know anything about love, I'm afraid. But I know what I like."

"It looks like gin," Simon said. He spread his cards on the table and smiled. "A nice early gin on a spade hand. What kind of cards are you holding, Granger?"

"Bad ones."

"Show 'em."

Marty spread his hand out while Simon counted the points. He was caught with twenty-three. That, plus the gin, doubled, added to ninety-six points; Simon tallied the score, then tapped the top of the table with the point of his pencil. "Puts me over in all three," he said. "With schneids in the second and third. You got hit bad, Granger."

"It looks that way."

"It does, Granger. It looks like maybe you don't play such a good game after all. You never should of raised the limit, Granger."

Marty didn't answer. He pushed the cards together and Simon began to shuffle them. The tide had turned, Marty thought. The thing was starting into a downhill slide. Simon had gotten almost even on the last game. He had to start putting the pressure on. At two dollars a point, Simon could ride a hot streak straight to the moon.

Simon put the pack on the table and Marty cut the cards. "Simon," he asked, "what do you do for a living?"

"I don't gamble. It's just a sideline with me."

"I figured that much. What do you do?"

"I buy and I sell."

"Stolen goods?"

Simon laughed this time. "Property," he said. "Real estate. Florida is nice that way. You buy something one day and sell it the next, and with the profit you make you can afford a lot of gin rummy. Hotels, restaurants, parking lots. I owned most of the Beach at one time or another. Not for long. I buy and I sell and I have a heavy turnover."

"It sounds interesting."

"It isn't. Pick up your cards, Granger. This time you get beat, and bad. I feel it."

Marty arranged his cards. He had a fair hand, not too good and not too bad. The up-card was the ten of diamonds. He took it, put it with two other tens, and let go of a king. Simon passed it up and drew the top card.

"This real estate," Marty said. "It pays nicely, huh?"

"Very nicely."

"You ever take a loss?"

"Now and then," Simon said. "You play a hard game and now and then you get your wings clipped. I had a hunk of vacant land, I bought it too high and I got strapped for cash. I wound up selling for a third of what I paid for the property."

"I just wondered."

Marty drew a queen and discarded it. Simon picked it up.

"I take a loss now and then," Simon said. "But not often. I come out ahead over the long haul, Granger. Way ahead."

The only bad time was right at the border. His nonchalance held. He stepped up along with a group of slightly drunk tourists who had just finished a madcap evening of whoring and drinking, and he followed them across the border. The guard on duty took a look at him, and something may have begun to register, but whatever it was it didn't connect completely. Weaver walked past the man and entered Texas.

Easy, he thought. Very easy. They were all idiots and he was smarter than any of them. He was the crafty killer, the clever werewolf, the brilliant vampire. They could never catch him.

A Mexican kid called to him, asking if he wanted his shoes shined. Why not, he thought. Something to do. And he might as well look sporty. He walked over to the kid and put one foot on the kid's shoebox. The boy whipped out a can of paste and a dirty rag and went to work on Weaver's shoe.

Poor kid, Weaver thought. Up at this hour shining shoes. Poor grubby Mexican kid.

While the boy polished the second shoe, he looked up at Weaver. His eyes looked several years older than the rest of his face. He asked Weaver if he would like to make love to his sister.

"No," Weaver said.

"She only twelve," the boy said. "She very good lay."

"Where is she?"

"Juarez."

Weaver thought about it. A twelve-year-old girl—now that would be very nice, very fine. But those Mex kids were all liars.

The girl probably wasn't twelve, was probably closer to twenty.

Besides, he didn't want to cross the border again. The whole point of crossing had been to kill in El Paso, so that he could have a victim on either side of the border in the same day. The boy's sister could wait for another day. There would be plenty of time for her later.

He told the kid to forget it, gave him a quarter for the shine and walked away down the street. The food smell from a diner reminded him that he was hungry. It occurred to him that someone in the diner might recognize him, but he decided to take the chance. They were all fools and idiots. They would not give him a second glance.

In the diner he ordered a hamburger steak with onions and a large glass of milk. He ate his meal and paid for it and left without tipping the waitress. And no one gave him a second glance.

He walked around, staying in the shadows, keeping his eyes open. He walked for a long time. When he stopped, finally, he stood shrouded in darkness at the entrance of the Warwick Hotel.

The bar was a quiet one. Meg nursed a glass of rum and Coca-Cola and listened to mariachi music on the battered juke box. She remembered her own words: I don't know anything about love, but I know what I like. Well, that was true enough. She didn't know where she was going or what she was doing, but she was having a hell of a time.

She knew what she liked. She liked Lily. The girl was a hard-boiled little creature and Meg didn't figure on sticking with her for very long, but while she kept her around she would have a lot of fun with her. The blonde knew wonderful ways to thrill Meg, and, after all, that was all that really mattered. Life was too short and people let it go too drab. You had to live for the thrills. There was little enough else to look forward to.

She set her rum Coke on the table and smoothed her black hair down with one hand. The record ended and blissful silence took its place. Suddenly she began to laugh. If only Borden Rector could have seen her a little while ago, if only he could have watched her in bed with Lily. That would have thrown him, all right. That would have knocked the stuffy bastard flat on his fat behind.

How long would it last with Lily? That was a good question, she told herself. It wouldn't be over too soon, because for the time being, at least, Lily was able to excite her as no one else could do. But she wasn't kidding herself. All Lily wanted out of the deal was a trip to New York with a pot of gold at the rainbow's end. And all she herself wanted was a thrill. When it ended, to hell with it.

I'm sex-mad, she thought. I'm a thrill girl with her brains between her legs.

And she smiled.

She lit a cigarette and smoked. She finished her rum Coke long after the ice had melted and the drink had gone to room temperature. She ordered another and sipped it slowly.

At a quarter to four she glanced upward and saw Lily. The blonde girl was smiling at her. A professional smile, Meg thought. But this didn't bother her.

"Like I'm ready, Meg."

"All set?"

"All set."

Outside, they walked a block until they came to one of the main streets. There Meg hailed a taxi and they sat together in the back seat. She told the driver to take them across the border to the Hotel Warwick. Then she leaned back to enjoy the ride.

On a whim she reached for Lily, and the girl came into her arms at once, ready to be kissed. Why not? Meg thought. Even in the back of the taxi, she was still in the driver's seat.

"It's just about four," Simon said. "You got to leave now, Granger. Remember what you said?"

"I remember."

"Your quitting time. You set it hours ago. Or did you change your mind, Granger?"

"I didn't change my mind."

"You owe me money, Granger."

Marty nodded. He checked the final score sheet. He was two thousand dollars behind, plus a few hundred. He took out his wallet and counted out bills in a flat voice. He put the precise sum on the table in front of Simon and the fat man looked at it with a happy expression on his face.

"You play lousy gin, Granger."

"Evidently."

"Never should of let me raise the limit. Bad policy, Granger, if you're money ahead, never let a man up the ante. It's a bad move."

"Thanks for the advice."

"It's nothing."

"That's the idea," Marty said. He stood up, shook his head. "I'll see you around," he told Simon. "You ever hit Paso again, be sure to look me up. Maybe we'll go around again."

"Fine. And when you're in Miami—"

"Yeah."

Marty walked to the door, opened it. It had been an expensive evening but the loss didn't even rankle him. He was tired now and felt strangely purged. The loss somehow atoned for the dissipation of the night before. There was a balance sheet somewhere, and he was even. In the hallway, he lit a cigarette and waited for the elevator.

And wondered. Where was she now? On a plane, two thousand miles off? Or just an elevator ride away?

The cab stopped across the street. Weaver saw them get out of it, the tall brunette and the short blonde. He had never seen the brunette before. But he recognized the blonde instantly. She was the one who had roomed next to him at Cappy's, the one he had wanted to kill there in the rundown hotel. He had missed his chance.

Now his chance had come back to him. It was fate, if ever anything was. Fate had brought him to this spot, at this moment. Fate had brought this woman back to him. She was meant to be his.

He whipped out the razor, flicked it open. They were crossing the street now and he was ready for them. It would have to be fast. He was taking a big chance, trying anything under conditions like these. But he had to take the chance, had to get the blonde—had to get both of them. He had no choice.

He waited as long as he dared. He waited, silent and still in the shadows, while they moved closer and closer to him. The brunette had her arm around the blonde and her hand was brushing the blonde's chunky breast. Weaver barely noticed this. He was too intent on Death to care about a brunette's hand on a blonde's breast.

He watched them slowly walk down the street, each tap of their heels bringing the two closer to him.

Weaver did not pay attention to the clicking sounds their heels made. He could only stare at their throats that shone white in the dim light of the coming dawn.

The two throats came closer and closer and he thought he

could see the blood pulsing through their jugular veins. But it was only the throbbing within his own body.

How could he do it?

He could suddenly leap out and with one broad sweep of his arm run the razor across both their throats. Then he could attack both of their bodies. He would slice off their clothes and then attack their breasts with the blade.

Weaver saw pink nipples turn bright red and then he saw the red, like molten lava from a volcano, gushing over soft white mounds.

One more step now would bring them to him. Only one more step.

He waited. And he sprang.

The blonde was nearer, and she died first, silently, without a scream. Weaver fell on her like a tree and his razor went for her throat. In a second she was on the ground with blood gushing from her slashed neck. The brunette leaped back in terror and screamed into the night.

But Weaver was too fast for her. He went after her and he caught her, and once again the razor went up and came down.

He did not stop when she died. He went on, using the razor like a club. He slashed again and again at the corpse of the brunette and he did not even stop when the man rushed out of the hotel and piled into him.

Marty hit the guy with everything he had. He had heard the screams while he was in the lobby and he came out on the run. He saw the blonde girl, dead, and he saw a little guy working on another woman. He went into action, hauling the guy away from her, sending a right crashing into the punk's face. He hit him five times and knocked him sprawling. Only when he got up and looked back did he see who it was the man had been attacking.

＊

In the police station, they told Marty he was a hero. They said the guy had killed two other women, one in Juarez and one in Paso, plus a little girl in Tulsa. They asked Marty if he knew either of the women who had been murdered in front of the hotel. He thought for a moment, about Meg, and told them no, that they were both strangers.

The newspaper boys took his name and his picture, and they told him he was a hero. They asked him if he knew about the fiend before. He told them he never read newspapers.

They let him go finally. He got into the blue Olds and started the motor. His whole mind was blank now. He thought of Meg, briefly, and then decided not to think of her anymore. She was dead. There was no point in thinking about her. *A gambler doesn't look back*. And he was a gambler. A professional.

He pulled the Olds onto the road and drove.

Away from the border. Away.

THE BURNING FURY

Originally published in the
February, 1959 issue of
OFF BEAT DETECTIVE STORIES

He was a big man with a rugged chin and the kind of eyes that could look right through a person, the piercing eyes that said, "I know who you are and I know your angle and I'm not buying it, so get out."

All of him said that—the solid frame without fat on it, the muscles in his arms, and even the way he was dressed. He wore a plaid flannel shirt open at the neck, a pair of tight blue jeans, and heavy logger's boots. Once the boots had been polished to a bright shine, but that was a long time ago. Now they were a dingy brown, scuffed and battered from plenty of hard wear.

He tossed off the shot of rotgut rye and sipped the beer chaser slowly, wondering how much of the slop he would pour down his gullet tonight. Christ, he was drinking too much. At this rate he'd drink himself broke by the time the season was up and he'd have to go bumming a ride to the next camp. And then it would just start in all over again—breaking your back over the big trees in the daytime and pouring down the rye and beer every night.

The days off were different. On those days it was cheap wine, half-a-buck-a-bottle Sneaky Pete, down the hatch the first thing in the morning and you kept right on with it until you passed out. That was on your day off, and you needed a day off like you needed a hole in your head.

When he worked he stayed sober until work was through for the day. He didn't need a drink while he was working, not with the full flavor of the open air racing through him and the joy of swinging that double-bit axe and working the big saw, not then.

Not when he was up on top, trimming her down and watching the axe bite through branches.

When he was working there was nothing to forget, no memories to grab him around the neck, no hungers to make him want to reach out and swing at somebody. Not when he had an axe in his hand.

But afterwards, then it was bad. Then the memories came, the Bad Things, and there had to be a way to forget them. The hunger came, stronger each time, and he couldn't sleep unless his gut was filled with whiskey or beer or wine or all three.

If only a man could work twenty-four hours a day...

He knew it would be bad the minute she came through the door. He saw her at once, saw the shape of her body and the color of her hair and the look in her eyes, and he knew right away that it was going to be one hell of a night. He took hold of the beer glass so hard he almost snapped it in two and tossed off the rest of the beer, calling for another shot with his next breath. The bartender came so slowly, and all the time he could see her out of the corner of his eye and feel the hunger come on like a sunset.

It was just like a sunset, the way his mind started going red and yellow and purple all at once and the way the hunger sat there like a big ball of fire nestling on the horizon. He closed his eyes and tried to black out the picture but it stayed with him, glowing and burning and sending hot shivers through his heavy body.

He told the bartender to make it a double, and he threw the double straight down and went to work on the beer chaser, hoping that the boilermakers would work tonight. Enough liquor would kill the sunset and put out the fire. It worked before. It had to work this time.

He watched her out of the corner of his eye, not wanting to

but not able to help himself. She was small—a good head shorter than he was, and she couldn't weigh half of what he did. But the weight she had was all placed just right, just the way he liked a woman to be put together.

Her hair was blonde—soft and fluffy and curling around her face like smoke. Her yellow sweater was just a shade deeper and brighter than her hair, and it showed off her body nicely, hugging and emphasizing the gentle curves.

The dark green skirt was tight, and it did things to the other half of her body.

He looked at her, and the ball of fire in his mind burned hotter and brighter every second.

Twenty or twenty-one, he guessed. Young, and with that innocent look that would stay with her no matter what she did or with whom or how often. He knew instinctively that the innocence was an illusion, and he would have known this if he saw her kneeling in a church instead of looking over the men in a logger's bar. But he knew at the same time that this was the only word for what she had: innocence. It was in the eyes, the way she moved, the half-smile on her full lips.

That was what did it: the youth, the innocence, the shape, and the knowledge that she was about as innocent as a Bowery fleabag. That did it every time, those four things all together, and he thought once again that this was going to be one hell of a night.

Another double followed the beer. It was beginning to take hold now, he noticed with a short sigh of relief. He rubbed a calloused finger over his right cheek and noted a sensation of numbness in his cheek, the first sign that the alcohol was reaching him. With his constant drinking it took a little more alcohol every night, but he was getting there now, getting to the point where the girl wouldn't affect him at all.

If only she'd give him time. Just a few more drinks and there would be nothing to worry about, a few more drinks and the numbness would spread slowly from his cheeks to the rest of his body and finally to his brain, quenching the yellow fire and letting him rest.

If only...

Out of the corner of his eye, he saw her eyes upon him, singling him out from the crowd at the bar. She took a hesitant step toward him and he wanted to shout "Go away!" at her. She kept on coming, and he wished that the stool on his right weren't empty, that with no place for her to sit she might leave him alone.

He finished the chaser and waved again for the bartender. Surely, inevitably, she walked to the bar and took the stool beside him. The dark green skirt caught on the stool and slithered up her leg as she sat, and the sight of firm white flesh heaped fresh fuel upon the mental ball of fire.

He tossed off the shot without tasting it or feeling any effect whatsoever. The beer followed the shot in one swallow, still bringing neither taste nor numbing peace. He winced as she tapped a cigarette twice on the polished surface of the bar and placed it between her lips.

The fumbling in her purse was, he knew, an act and nothing more. Christ, they were all the same, every one of them. He could even time the pitch—it would come on the count of three. One. Two. Thr—

"Do you have a match?"

Right on schedule. He ignored her, concentrating instead on the drink that had appeared magically before him. He hardly remembered ordering it. He couldn't remember anything anymore, not since she took the seat beside him, not since every bit of his concentration had been devoted to her.

"A match, please?"

He pulled a box of wooden matches from his shirt pocket without thinking, scratched one on the underside of the bar and held it to her cigarette. She leaned toward him to take the light, moving her leg slightly against his, touching him briefly before withdrawing.

Right on schedule.

He closed the matchbox and stuffed it back into his shirt pocket, trying to force his attention back to the drink in front of him. His fingers closed around the shot glass. But he couldn't even seem to lift it from the bar, couldn't raise the drink that might save him for that night at least.

He wanted to turn to her and snarl: *Look, I'm not interested. I don't care if it's for sale or free for the taking, I'm not interested. Take your hot little body and get the hell out.*

But he didn't even turn around. He sat still, his heavy frame motionless on the stool; waiting for what had to come next.

"You're lonesome aren't you?"

He didn't answer. Christ, even her voice had that sugary innocence, that mixture of sex and baby powder. It was funny he hadn't noticed it before, and he wished he hadn't noticed it now. It just made everything so much worse.

"You're lonesome." It was a statement now, almost a command.

"No, I'm not." Instantly he hated himself for answering at all. The words came from his lips almost by themselves, without him wishing it at all.

"Of course you are. I can tell." She spoke as if she were completely sure of herself, and as she talked her body moved imperceptibly closer to him, her leg inching toward his and pressing against it firmly, not withdrawing this time but remaining there, inflaming him.

His fingers squeezed the shot glass but it stayed on the bar, the rye out of his reach when he needed it so badly.

"Go away." He meant to snap the words at her like axe-blows, but instead, they dribbled almost inaudibly from his lips.

"You're lonesome and unhappy. I know."

"Look, I'm fine. Why don't you go bother somebody else?"

She smiled. "You don't mean that," she said. "You don't mean that at all. Besides, I don't want to bother anybody else, can't you see? I want to be with you."

"Why?"

"Because you're big. I like big men."

Sure, he thought. It was like this all the time. "There's other big guys around."

"Not like you. You got that sad lonesome look, like I can see it a mile away how lonesome you are. And unhappy, you know. It sticks out."

It did; that much was true enough.

"Look," she was saying, "what are you fighting for, huh? You're lonesome and I'm here. You're unhappy and I can make you happy."

When he hesitated, she explained: "I'm good at making guys happy. You'd be surprised."

"I'll bet you are." Christ, why couldn't he just shut up and let her talk herself dry? No, he had to go on making small talk and feeling that hot little leg digging into his and listening to that syrupy voice dripping into his ear like maple syrup into a tin cup. He had to glance at her every second out of the corner of his eye, drinking in the softness of her. His nostrils were filled with the smell of her, a smell that was a mixture of cheap perfume and warm woman-smell, an odor that got into his bloodstream and just made everything worse than ever.

"I can make you happy."

He didn't answer, thinking how happy she would make him if she would just leave now, right away, if the earth would only open up and swallow her or him or both of them, just so long as she would leave him alone. There wasn't much time left.

"Look."

He turned his head involuntarily and watched her wiggle slightly in place, her body moving and rubbing against the sweater and skirt.

"It's all me," she explained. "Under the clothes, I mean."

He clenched his teeth and said nothing.

"I'll make you happy," she said again. When he didn't reply she placed her hand gently on his and repeated the four words in a half-whisper. Her hand was so small, so small and soft.

"C'mon," she said.

He stood up and followed her out the door, the glass of rye still untouched.

She said her place wasn't far and they walked in the direction she led him, away from the center of town. He didn't say anything all the way, and she only repeated her promise to make him happy. She said it over and over as if it were a magic phrase, a charm of some sort.

His arm went around her automatically and his hand squeezed the firm flesh of her waist. There was no holding back any-more—he knew that, and he didn't try to stop his fingers from gently kneading the flesh or the other hand from reaching for hers and enveloping it possessively. This act served to bring her body right up next to his so that they bumped together with every step. After a block or so her head nestled against his shoulder and remained there for the rest of the walk. The fluffy blonde hair brushed against his cheek.

The cheek wasn't numb anymore.

It was cold out but he didn't notice the cold. It was windy, but he didn't feel the wind cut through the tight blue jeans and the flannel shirt. She had lied slightly: it was a long walk to her place, but he didn't even notice the distance.

She lived by herself in a little shack, a tossed-together affair of unpainted planks with nails knocked in crudely. Somebody had tried to get a garden growing in front but the few plants were all dead now and the weeds overran the small patch. He knew, seeing the shack, why she had fixed on the idea of him being lonely. She was so obviously alone, living off by herself and away from the rest of the world.

Inside, she closed and bolted the door and turned to him, her eyes expectant and her mouth waiting to be kissed. He closed his eyes briefly. Maybe he could open them and discover that she wasn't there at all, that he was back at the bar by himself or maybe out cold in his own cabin.

But she was still there when he opened his eyes. She was still standing close to him, her mouth puckered and her eyes vaguely puzzled.

"I'll make you happy." She said those four words as if they were the answer to every question in the universe, and by this time he thought that perhaps they were.

There was no other answer.

He clenched his teeth again, just as he had done when she squirmed before him on the barstool. Then he drove one fist into her stomach and watched her double up in pain, the physical pain of the blow more than matched by the hurt and confusion in her eyes.

He struck her again, a harsh slap on the side of her face that sent her reeling. She started to fall and he brought his knee up, catching her on the jaw and breaking several of her teeth. He hauled her to her feet and the sweater ripped away like tissue paper.

She was right. It was all her underneath.

The next slap started her crying. The one after that knocked the wind out of her and stopped her tears for the time being. His fingers ripped at the skirt and one of his nails dug at her skin, drawing blood. She crumpled to the floor, her whole body shaking with terror and pain, and he fell upon her greedily.

The bitch, he thought. The stupid little bitch.

Couldn't she guess there was only one way to make him happy?

A FIRE AT NIGHT

*Originally published in the
June, 1958 issue of MANHUNT*

He gazed silently into the flame. The old tenement was burning, and the smoke was rising upward to merge against the blackness of the sky. There were neither stars nor moon in the sky, and the street lights in the neighborhood were dim and spaced far apart. Nothing detracted from the brilliance of the fire. It stood out against the night like a diamond in a pot of bubbling tar. It was a beautiful fire.

He looked around and smiled. The crowd was growing larger, as everyone in the area thronged together to watch the building burn. They like it, he thought. Everyone likes a fire. They receive pleasure from staring into the flames, watching them dance on the tenement roof. But their pleasure could never match his, for it was his fire. It was the most beautiful fire he had ever set.

His mind filled with the memory of it. It had been planned to perfection. When the sun dropped behind the tall buildings and the sky grew dark, he had placed the can of kerosene in his car with the rags—plain, non-descript rags that could never be traced to him. And then he had driven to the old tenement. The lock on the cellar door was no problem, and there was no one around to get in the way. The rags were placed, the kerosene was spread, the match was struck, and he was on his way. In seconds the flames were licking at the ancient walls and racing up the staircases.

The fire had come a long way now. It looked as though the building had a good chance of caving in before the blaze was extinguished. He hoped vaguely that the building would fall. He wanted his fire to win.

He glanced around again, and was amazed at the size of the crowd. All of them pressed close, watching his fire. He wanted to call to them. He wanted to scream out that it was his fire, that he and he alone had created it. With effort he held himself back. If he cried out it would be the end of it. They would take him away and he would never set another fire.

Two of the firemen scurried to the tenement with a ladder. He squinted at them, and recognized them—Joe Dakin and Roger Haig. He wanted to call hello to them, but they were too far away to hear him. He didn't know them well, but he felt as though he did. He saw them quite often.

He watched Joe and Roger set the ladder against the side of the building. Perhaps there was someone trapped inside. He remembered the other time when a small boy had failed to leave the building in time. He could still hear the screams— loud at first, then softer until they died out to silence. But this time he thought the building had been empty.

The fire was beautiful! It was warm and soft as a woman. It sang with life and roared with joy. It seemed almost a person, with a mind and a will of its own.

Joe Dakin started up the ladder. Then there must be someone in the building. Someone had not left in time and was trapped with the fire. That was a shame. If only there were a way for him to warn them! Perhaps next time he could give them a tele- phone call as soon as the blaze was set.

Of course, there was even a beauty in trapping someone in the building. A human sacrifice to the fire, an offering to the goddess of Beauty. The pain, the loss of life was unfortunate, but the beauty was compensation. He wondered who might be caught inside.

Joe Dakin was almost to the top of the ladder. He stopped at a window on the fifth floor and looked inside. The he climbed through.

Joe is brave, he thought. I hope he isn't hurt. I hope he saves the person in the building.

He turned around. There was a little man next to him, a little man in shabby clothes with a sad expression on his face. He reached over and tapped the man on the shoulder.

"Hey!" he said. "You know who's in the building?"

The little man nodded wordlessly.

"Who is it?"

"Mrs. Pelton," said the little man. "Morris Pelton's mother."

He had never heard of Morris Pelton. "Well, Joe'll get her out. Joe's a good fireman."

The little man shook his head. "Can't get her out," he said. "Can't nobody get her out."

He felt irritated. Who was this little jerk to tell him? "What do you mean?" he said. "I tell you Joe's a helluva fireman. He'll take care of it."

The little man flashed him a superior look. "She's fat," he said. "She's a real big woman. She must weigh two hundred pounds easy. This Joe's just a little guy. How's he gonna get her out? Huh?" The little man tossed his head triumphantly and turned away without an answer.

Another sacrifice, he thought. Joe would be disappointed. He'd want to rescue the woman, but she would die in the fire.

He looked at the window. Joe should come out soon. He couldn't save Mrs. Pelton, and in a few seconds he would be coming down the ladder. And then the fire would burn and burn and burn, until the walls of the building crumbled and caved in, and the fire won the battle. The smoke would curl in ribbons from the ashes. It would be wonderful to watch.

He looked up at the window suddenly. Something was wrong. Joe was there at last, but he had the woman with him. Was he out of his mind?

The little man had not exaggerated. The woman was big,

much larger than Joe. He could barely see Joe behind her, holding her in his arms. Joe couldn't sling her into a fireman's carry; she would have broken his back.

He shuddered. Joe was going to try to carry her down the ladder, to cheat the fire of its victim. He held her as far from his body as he could and reached out a foot gingerly. His foot found the first rung and rested on it.

He took his other foot from the windowsill and reached out for the next rung. He held tightly to the woman, who was screaming now. Her body shook with each scream, and rolls of fat bounced up and down.

The damned fool, he thought. How could he expect to haul a fat slob like that down five flights on a ladder? He was a good fireman, but he didn't have to act like a superman. And the bitch didn't even know what was going on. She just kept screaming her head off. Joe was risking his neck for her, and she didn't even appreciate it at all.

He looked at Joe's face as the fireman took another halting step. Joe didn't look good. He had been inside the building too long. The smoke was bothering him.

Joe took another step and tottered on the ladder. Drop her, he thought. You goddamned fool, let go of her!

And then he did. The woman slipped suddenly from Joe's grip, and plummeted downward to the sidewalk. Her scream rose higher and higher as she fell, and then stopped completely. She struck the pavement like a bug smacking against the windshield of a car.

His whole being filled with relief. Thank God, he thought. It was too bad for the woman, but now Joe would reach the ground safely. But he noticed that Joe seemed to be in trouble. He was still swaying back and forth. He was coughing, too.

And then, all at once, Joe fell. He left the ladder and began to drop to the earth. His body hovered in the air and floated down like a feather. Then he hit the ground and melted into the pavement.

At first he could not believe it. Then he glared at the fire. Damn you, he thought. You weren't satisfied with the old woman. You had to take a fireman too.

It wasn't right.

The fire was evil. This time it had gone too far. Now it would have to suffer for it.

And then he raised his hose and trained it on the burning hulk of the tenement, punishing the fire.

STAG PARTY GIRL

Originally published in the
February, 1963 issue of MAN'S MAGAZINE

I

Harold Merriman pushed his chair back and stood up, drink in hand. "Gentlemen," he said solemnly, "to all the wives we love so well. May they continue to belong to us body and soul." He paused theatrically. "And to their husbands—may they never find out!"

There was scattered laughter, most of it lost in the general hubbub. I had a glass of cognac on the table in front of me. I took a sip and looked at Mark Donahue. If he was nervous, it didn't show. He looked like any man who was getting married in the morning—which is nervous enough, I suppose. He didn't look like someone threatened with murder.

Phil Abeles—short, intense, brittle-voiced—stood. He started to read a sheaf of fake telegrams. "Mark," he intoned, "don't panic—marriage is the best life for a man. Signed, Tommy Manville…" He read more telegrams. Some funny, some mildly obscene, some dull.

We were in an upstairs dining room at McGraw's, a venerable steakhouse in the East Forties. About a dozen of us. There was Mark Donahue, literally getting married in the morning, Sunday, tying the nuptial knot at 10:30. Also Harold Merriman, Phil Abeles, Ray Powell, Joe Conn, Jack Harris and a few others whose names I couldn't remember, all fellow wage slaves with Donahue at Darcy & Bates, one of Madison Avenue's rising young ad agencies.

And there was me. Ed London, private cop, the man at the party who didn't belong. I was just a hired hand. It was my job to get Donahue to the church on time, and alive.

On Wednesday, Mark Donahue had come to my apartment. He cabbed over on a long lunch hour that coincided with the time I rolled out of bed. We sat in my living room. I was rumpled and ugly in a moth-eaten bathrobe. He was fresh and trim in a Tripler suit and expensive shoes. I drowned my sorrows with coffee while he told me his problems.

"I think I need a bodyguard," he said.

In the storybooks and the movies, I show him the door at this point. I explain belligerently that I don't do divorce or bodyguard work or handle corporate investigations—that I only rescue stacked blondes and play modern-day Robin Hood. That's in the storybooks. I don't play that way. I have an apartment in an East Side brownstone and I eat in good restaurants and drink expensive cognac. If you can pay my fee, friend, you can buy me.

I asked him what it was all about.

"I'm getting married Sunday morning," he said.

"Congratulations."

"Thanks." He looked at the floor. "I'm marrying a…a very fine girl. Her name is Lynn Farwell."

I waited.

"There was another girl I…used to see. A model, more or less. Karen Price."

"And?"

"She doesn't want me to get married."

"So?"

He fumbled for a cigarette. "She's been calling me," he said. "I was…well, fairly deeply involved with her. I never planned to marry her. I'm sure she knew that."

"But you were sleeping with her?"

"That's right."

"And now you're marrying someone else."

He sighed at me. "It's not as though I ruined the girl," he said. "She's...well, not a tramp, exactly, but close to it. She's been around, London."

"So what's the problem?"

"I've been getting phone calls from her. Unpleasant ones, I'm afraid. She's told me that I'm not going to marry Lynn. That she'll see me dead first."

"And you think she'll try to kill you?"

"I don't know."

"That kind of threat is common, you know. It doesn't usually lead to murder."

He nodded hurriedly. "I know that," he said. "I'm not terribly afraid she'll kill me. I just want to make sure she doesn't throw a monkey wrench into the wedding. Lynn comes from an excellent family. Long Island, society, money. Her parents wouldn't appreciate a scene."

"Probably not."

He forced a little laugh. "And there's always a chance that she really may try to kill me," he said. "I'd like to avoid that." I told him it was an understandable desire. "So I want a bodyguard. From now until the wedding. Four days. Will you take the job?"

I told him my fee ran a hundred a day plus expenses. This didn't faze him. He gave me $300 for a retainer, and I had a client and he had a bodyguard.

From then on I stuck to him like perspiration.

Saturday, a little after noon, he got a phone call. We were playing two-handed pinochle in his living room. He was winning. The phone rang and he answered it. I only heard his end of the conversation. He went a little white and sputtered; then he stood for a long moment with the phone in his hand, and finally slammed the receiver on the hook and turned to me.

"Karen," he said, ashen. "She's going to kill me."

I didn't say anything. I watched the color come back into his face, saw the horror recede. He came up smiling. "I'm not really scared," he said.

"Good."

"Nothing's going to happen," he added. "Maybe it's her idea of a joke…maybe she's just being bitchy. But nothing's going to happen."

He didn't entirely believe it. But I had to give him credit.

I don't know who invented the bachelor dinner, or why he bothered. I've been to a few of them. Dirty jokes, dirty movies, dirty toasts, a line-up with a local whore—maybe I would appreciate them if I were married. But for a bachelor who makes out there is nothing duller than a bachelor dinner.

This one was par for the course. The steaks were good and there was a lot to drink, which was definitely on the plus side. The men busy making asses of themselves were not friends of mine, and that was also on the plus side—it kept me from getting embarrassed for them. But the jokes were still unfunny and the voices too drunkenly loud.

I looked at my watch. "Eleven-thirty," I said to Donahue. "How much longer do you think this'll go on?"

"Maybe half an hour."

"And then ten hours until the wedding. Your ordeal's just about over, Mark."

"And you can relax and spend your fee."

"Uh-huh."

"I'm glad I hired you," he said. "You haven't had to do anything, but I'm glad anyway." He grinned. "I carry life insurance, too. But that doesn't mean I'm going to die. And you've even been good company, Ed. Thanks."

I started to search for an appropriate answer. Phil Abeles

saved me. He was standing up again, pounding on the table with his fist and shouting for everyone to be quiet. They let him shout for a while, then quieted down.

"And now the grand finale," Phil announced wickedly. "The part I know you've all been waiting for."

"The part Mark's been waiting for," someone said lewdly.

"Mark better watch this," someone else added. "He has to learn about women so that Lynn isn't disappointed."

More feeble lines, one after the other. Phil Abeles pounded for order again and got it. "Lights," he shouted.

The lights went out. The private dining room looked like a blackout in a coal mine.

"Music!"

Somewhere, a record player went on. The record was *Stripper,* played by David Rose's orchestra.

"Action!"

A spotlight illuminated the pair of doors at the far end of the room. The doors opened. Two bored waiters wheeled in a large table on rollers. There was a cardboard cake on top of the table and, obviously, a girl inside the cake. Somebody made a joke about Mark cutting himself a piece. Someone else said they wanted to put a piece of this particular wedding cake under their pillow. "On the pillow would be better," a voice corrected.

The two bored waiters wheeled the cake into position and left.

The doors closed. The spotlight stayed on the cake and the stripper music swelled.

There were two or three more lame jokes. Then the chatter died. Everyone seemed to be watching the cake. The music grew louder, deeper, fuller. The record stopped suddenly and another—Mendelsohn's *Wedding March*—took its place.

Someone shouted, "Here comes the bride!"

And she leaped out of the cake like a nymph from the sea.

She was naked and beautiful. She sprang through the paper cake, arms wide, face filled with a lipstick smile. Her breasts were full and firm and her nipples had been reddened with lipstick.

Then, just as everyone was breathlessly silent, just as her arms spread and her lips parted and her eyes widened slightly, the whole room exploded like Hiroshima. We found out later that it was only a .38. It sounded more like a howitzer.

She clapped both hands to a spot between her breasts. Blood spurted forth like a flower opening. She gave a small gasp, swayed forward, then dipped backward and fell.

Lights went on. I raced forward. Her head was touching the floor and her legs were propped on what remained of the paper cake. Her eyes were open. But she was horribly dead.

And then I heard Mark Donahue next to me, his voice shrill. "Oh, no!" he said. "…It's Karen, it's Karen!"

I felt for a pulse; there was no point to it. There was a bullet in her heart.

Karen Price was dead.

2

Lieutenant Jerry Gunther got the call. He brought a clutch of Homicide men who went around measuring things, studying the position of the body, shooting off a hell of a lot of flashbulbs and taking statements. Jerry piloted me into a corner and started pumping.

I gave him the whole story, starting with Wednesday and ending with Saturday. He let me go all the way through once, then went over everything two or three times.

"Your client Donahue doesn't look too good," he said.

"You think he killed the girl?"

"That's the way it reads."

I shook my head. "Wrong customer."

"Why?"

"Hell, he hired me to keep the girl off his neck. If he was going to shoot a hole in her, why would he want a detective along for company?"

"To make the alibi stand up, Ed. To make us reason just the way you're reasoning now. How do you know he was scared of the girl?"

"Because he said so. But—"

"But he got a phone call?" Jerry smiled. "For all you know it was a wrong number. Or the call had been staged. You only heard his end of it. Remember?"

"I saw his face when he took a good look at the dead girl," I said. "Mark Donahue was one surprised hombre, Jerry. He didn't know who she was."

"Or else he's a good actor."

"Not that good. I can't believe it."

He let that one pass. "Let's go back to the shooting," he said. "Were you watching him when the gun went off?"

"No."

"What were you watching?"

"The girl," I said. "And quit grinning, you fathead."

His grin spread. "You old lecher. All right, you can't alibi him for the shooting. And you can't prove he was afraid of the girl. This is the way I make it, Ed. He was afraid of her, but not afraid she would kill him. He was afraid of something else. Call it blackmail, maybe. He's getting set to make a good marriage to a rich doll and he's got a mistress hanging around his neck. Say the rich girl doesn't know about the mistress. Say the mistress wants hush money."

"Go on."

"Your Donahue finds out the Price doll is going to come out of the cake."

"They kept it a secret from him, Jerry."

"Sometimes people find out secrets. The Price kid could have told him herself. It might have been her idea of a joke. Say he finds out. He packs a gun—"

"He didn't have a gun."

"How do you know, Ed?"

I couldn't answer that one. He might have had a gun. He might have tucked it into a pocket while he was getting dressed. I didn't believe it, but I couldn't disprove it either.

Jerry Gunther was thorough. He didn't have to be thorough to turn up the gun. It was under a table in the middle of the room. The lab boys checked it for prints. None. It was a .38 police positive with five bullets left in it. The bullets didn't have any prints on them, either.

"Donahue shot her, wiped the gun and threw it on the floor," Jerry said.

"Anybody else could have done the same thing," I interjected.

"Uh-huh. Sure."

He grilled Phil Abeles, the man who had hired Karen Price to come out of the cake. Abeles was also the greenest, sickest man in the world at that particular moment.

Gunther asked him how he got hold of the girl. "I never knew anything about her," Abeles insisted. "I didn't even know her last name."

"How'd you find her?"

"A guy gave me her name and her number. When I…when we set up the dinner, the stag, we thought we would have a wedding cake with a girl jumping out of it. We thought it would be so…so corny that it might be cute. You know?"

No one said anything. Abeles was sweating up a storm. The dinner had been his show and it had not turned out as he had planned it, and he looked as though he wanted to go somewhere quiet and die. "So I asked around to find out where to get a girl," he went on. "Honest, I asked a dozen guys, two dozen. I don't know how many. I asked everybody in this room except Mark. I asked half the guys on Madison Avenue. Someone gave me a number, told me to call it and ask for Karen. So I did. She said she'd jump out of the cake for $100 and I said that was fine."

"You didn't know she was Donahue's mistress?"

"Oh, brother," he said. "You have to be kidding." We told him we weren't kidding. He got greener.

"Maybe that made it a better joke," I suggested. "To have Mark's girl jump out of the cake the night before he married someone else. Was that it?"

"Hell, no!"

Jerry grilled everyone in the place. No one admitted knowing Karen Price, or realized that she had been involved with Mark Donahue. No one admitted anything. Most of the men were married. They were barely willing to admit that they were alive. Some of them were almost as green as Phil Abeles.

They wanted to go home. That was all they wanted. They kept mentioning how nice it would be if their names didn't get into the papers. Some of them tried a little genteel bribery. Jerry was tactful enough to pretend he didn't know what they were talking about. He was an honest cop. He didn't do favors and didn't take gifts.

By 1:30, he had sent them all home. The lab boys were still making chalk marks but there wasn't much point to it. According to their measurements and calculations of the bullet's trajectory, and a few other scientific bits and pieces, they managed to prove conclusively that Karen Price had been shot by someone in McGraw's private dining room.

And that was all they could prove.

Four of us rode down to Headquarters at Centre Street. Mark Donahue sat in front, silent. Jerry Gunther sat on his right. A beardless cop named Ryan, Jerry's driver, had the wheel. I occupied the back seat all alone.

At Fourteenth Street Mark broke his silence. "This is a nightmare. I didn't kill Karen. Why in God's name would I kill her?"

Nobody had an answer for him. A few blocks further he said, "I suppose I'll be railroaded now. I suppose you'll lock me up and throw the key away."

Gunther told him, "We don't railroad people. We couldn't if we wanted to. We don't have enough of a case yet. But right now you look like a pretty good suspect. Figure it out for yourself."

"But—"

"I have to lock you up, Donahue. You can't talk me out of it. Ed can't talk me out of it. Nobody can."

"I'm supposed to get married tomorrow."

"I'm afraid that's out."

The car moved south. For a while nobody had anything to say.

A few blocks before Police Headquarters Mark told me he wanted me to stay on the case.

"You'll be wasting your money," I told him. "The police will work things out better than I can. They have the manpower and the authority. I'll just be costing you a hundred a day and getting you nothing in return."

"Are you trying to talk yourself out of a fee?"

"He's an ethical bastard," Jerry put in. "In his own way, of course."

"I want you working for me, Ed."

"Why?"

He waited a minute, organizing his thoughts. "Look," he sighed, "do you think I killed Karen?"

"No."

"Honestly?"

"Honestly."

"Well, that's one reason I want you in my corner. Maybe the police are fair in these things. I don't know anything about it. But they'll be looking for things that'll nail me. They have to— it's their job. From where they sit I'm the killer." He paused, as if the thought stunned him a little. "But you'll be looking for something that will help me. Maybe you can find someone who was looking at me when the gun went off. Maybe you can figure out who did pull that trigger and why. I know I'll feel better if you're working for me."

"Don't expect anything."

"I don't."

"I'll do what I can," I told him.

Before I caught a cab from Headquarters to my apartment, I told Mark to call his lawyer. He wouldn't be able to get out on bail because there is no bail in first-degree murder cases; but a lawyer could do a lot of helpful things for him. Lynn Farwell's family had to be told that there wasn't going to be a wedding.

I don't envy anyone who has to call a mother or father at 3 A.M. and explain that their daughter's wedding, set for 10:30 that very morning, must be postponed because the potential bride-groom has been arrested for murder.

I sat back in the cab with an unlit pipe in my mouth and a lot of aimless thoughts rumbling around in my head. Nothing made much sense yet. Perhaps nothing ever would. It was that kind of a deal.

3

Morning was noisy, ugly and several hours premature. A sharp, persistent ringing stabbed my brain into a semiconscious state. I cursed and groped for the alarm clock, turned it off. The buzzing continued. I reached for the phone, lifted the receiver to my ear, and listened to a dial tone. The buzzing continued. I cursed even more vehemently and stumbled out of bed. I found a bathrobe and groped into it. I splashed cold water on my face and blinked at myself in the mirror. I looked as bad as I felt.

The doorbell kept ringing. I didn't want to answer it, but that seemed the only way to make it stop ringing. I listened to my bones creak on the way to the door. I turned the knob, opened the door and blinked at the blonde who was standing there. She blinked back at me.

"Mister," she said. "You look terrible."

She didn't. Even at that ghastly hour she looked like a toothpaste ad. Her hair was blonde silk and her eyes were blue jewels and her skin was creamed perfection. With a thinner body and a more severe mouth she could have been a *Vogue* model. But the body was just too bountiful for the fashion magazines. The breasts were a perfect 38, high and large, the waist trim, the hips a curved invitation.

"You're Ed London?"

I nodded foolishly.

"I'm Lynn Farwell."

She didn't have to tell me. She looked exactly like what my client had said he was going to marry, except a little better.

Everything about her stated emphatically that she was from Long Island's North Shore, that she had gone to an expensive finishing school and a ritzy college, that her family had half the money in the world.

"May I come in?"

"You got me out of bed," I grumbled.

"I'm sorry. I wanted to talk to you."

"Could you sort of go somewhere and come back in about ten minutes? I'd like to get human."

"I don't really have any place to go. May I just sit in your living room or something? I'll be quiet."

There is a pair of matching overstuffed leather chairs in my living room, the kind they have in British men's clubs. She curled up and got lost in one of them. I left her there and ducked back into the bedroom. I showered, shaved, dressed. When I came out again the world was a somewhat better place. I smelled coffee.

"I put up a pot of java." She smiled. "Hope you don't mind."

"I couldn't mind less," I said. We waited while the coffee dripped through. I poured out two cups, and we both drank it black.

"I haven't seen Mark," she said. "His lawyer called. I suppose you know all about it, of course."

"More or less."

"I'll be seeing Mark later this afternoon, I suppose. We were supposed to be getting married in—" she looked at her watch "—a little over an hour."

She seemed unperturbed. There were no tears, not in her eyes and not in her voice. She asked me if I was still working for Donahue. I nodded.

"He didn't kill that girl," she said.

"I don't think he did."

"I'm sure. Of all the ridiculous things... Why did he hire you, Ed?"

I thought a moment and decided to tell her the truth. She probably knew it anyway. Besides, there was no point in sparing her the knowledge that her fiancé had a mistress somewhere along the line. That should be the least of her worries, compared to a murder rap.

It was. She greeted the news with a half-smile and shook her head sadly. "Now why on earth would they think she could blackmail him?" Lynn Farwell demanded. "I don't care who he slept with... Policemen are asinine."

I didn't say anything. She sipped her coffee, stretched a little in the chair, crossed one leg over the other. She had very nice legs.

We both lit cigarettes. She blew out a cloud of smoke and looked at me through it, her blue eyes narrowing. "Ed," she said, "how long do you think it'll be before he's cleared?"

"It's impossible to say, Miss Farwell."

"Lynn."

"Lynn. It could take a day or a month."

She nodded thoughtfully. "He has to be cleared as quickly as possible. That's the most important thing. There can't be any scandal, Ed. Oh, a little dirt is bearable. But nothing serious, nothing permanent."

Something didn't sound right. She didn't care who he slept with, but no scandal could touch them—this was vitally important to her. She sounded like anything but a loving bride-to-be.

She read my mind. "I don't sound madly in love, do I?"

"Not particularly."

She smiled kittenishly. "I'd like more coffee, Ed..."

I got more for both of us.

Then she said, "Mark and I don't love each other, Ed."

I grunted noncommittally.

"We like each other, though. I'm fond of Mark, and he's fond of me. That's all that matters, really."

"Is it?"

She nodded positively. Finishing schools and high-toned colleges produce girls with the courage of their convictions. "It's enough," she said. "Love's a poor foundation for marriage in the long run. People who love are too...too vulnerable. Mark and I are perfect for each other. We'll both be getting something out of this marriage."

"What will Mark get?"

"A rich wife. A proper connection with an important family. That's what he wants."

"And you?"

"A respectable marriage to a promising young man."

"If that's all you want—"

"It's all I want," she said. "Mark is good company. He's bright, socially acceptable, ambitious enough to be stimulating. He'll make a good husband and a good father. I'm happy."

She yawned again and her body uncoiled in the chair. The movement drew her breasts into sharp relief against the front of her sweater. This was supposed to be accidental. I knew better.

"Besides," she said, her voice just slightly husky, "he's not at all bad in bed."

I wanted to slap her well-bred face. The lips were slightly parted now, her eyes a little less than half lidded. The operative term I think, is *provocative.* She knew damned well what she was doing with the coy posing and the sex talk and all the rest. She had the equipment to carry it off, too. But it was a horrible hour on a horrible Sunday morning, and her fiancé was also my client, and he was sitting in a cell, booked on suspicion of homicide.

So I neither took her to bed nor slapped her face. I let the remark die in the stuffy air and finished my second cup of coffee. There was a rack of pipes on the table next to my chair. I selected a sandblast Barling and stuffed some tobacco into it. I lit it and smoked.

"Ed?"

I looked at her.

"I didn't mean to sound cheap."

"Forget it."

"All right." A pause. "Ed, you'll find a way to clear Mark, won't you?"

"I'll try."

"If there's any way I can help—"

"I'll let you know."

She gave me her phone number and address. She was living with her parents.

Then she paused at the door and turned enough to let me look at her lovely young body in profile. "If there's anything you want," she said softly, "be sure to let me know."

It was an ordinary enough line. But I had the feeling that it covered a lot of ground.

At 11:30 I picked up my car at the garage around the corner from my apartment.

The car is a Chevy convertible, an old one that dates from the pre-fin era. I left the top up. The air had an edge to it. I took the East Side Drive downtown and pulled up across the street from Headquarters at noon.

They let me see Mark Donahue. He was wearing the same expensive suit but it didn't hang right now. It looked as though it had been slept in, which figured. He needed a shave and his eyes had red rims. I didn't ask him how he had slept. I could tell.

"Hello," he said.

"Getting along all right?"

"I suppose so." He swallowed. "They asked me questions most of the night. No rubber hose, though. That's something."

"Sure," I said. "Mind some more questions?"

"Go ahead."

"When did you start seeing Karen Price?"

"Four, five months ago."

"When did you stop?"

"About a month ago."

"Why?"

"Because I was practically married to Lynn."

"Who knew you were sleeping with Karen?"

"No one I know of."

"Anybody at the stag last night?"

"I don't think so."

More questions. When had she started phoning him? About two weeks ago, maybe a little longer than that. Was she in love with him? He hadn't thought so, no, and that was why the phone calls were such a shock to him at first. As far as he was concerned, it was just a mutual sex arrangement with no emotional involvement on either side. He took her to shows, bought her presents, gave her occasional small loans with the understanding that they weren't to be repaid. He wasn't exactly keeping her and she wasn't exactly going to bed in return for the money. It was just a convenient arrangement.

Everything, it seemed, was just a convenient arrangement. He and Karen Price had had a convenient shack-up. He and Lynn Farwell were planning a convenient marriage.

But someone had put a bullet in Karen's pretty chest. People don't do that because it's convenient. They usually have more emotional reasons.

More questions. Where did Karen live? He gave me an address

in the Village, not too very far from his own apartment. Who were her friends? He knew one, her roommate, Ceil Gorski. Where did she work? He wasn't too clear.

"My lawyer's trying to get them to reduce the charge," he said. "So that I can get out on bail. You think he'll manage it?"

"He might."

"I hope so," he said. His face went serious, then brightened again. "This is a hell of a place to spend a wedding night," he smiled. "Funny—when I was trying to pick the right hotel, I never thought of a jail."

4

It was only a few blocks from Mark Donahue's cell to the building where Karen Price had lived...a great deal further in terms of dollars and cents. She had an apartment in a red-brick five-story building on Sullivan Street, just below Bleecker.

The girl who opened the door was blonde, like Lynn Farwell. But her dark roots showed and her eyebrows were dark brown. If her mouth and eyes relaxed she would have been pretty. They didn't.

"You just better not be another cop," she said.

"I'm afraid I am. But not city. Private."

The door started to close. I made like a brush salesman and tucked a foot in it. She glared at me.

"Private cops, I don't have to see," she said. "Get the hell out, will you?"

"I just want to talk to you."

"The feeling isn't mutual. Look—"

"It won't take long."

"You son of a bitch," she said. But she opened the door and let me inside. We walked through the kitchen to the living room. There was a couch there. She sat on it. I took a chair. "Who are you anyway?" she said.

"My name's Ed London."

"Who you working for?"

"Mark Donahue."

"The one who killed her?"

"I don't think he did," I said. "What I'm trying to find out, Miss Gorski, is who did."

She got to her feet and started walking around the room. There was nothing deliberately sexy about her walk. She was hard, though. She lived in a cheap apartment on a bad block. She bleached her hair, and her hairdresser wasn't the only one who knew for sure. She could have—but didn't—come across as a slut.

There was something honest and forthright about her, if not necessarily wholesome. She was a big blonde with a hot body and a hard face. There are worse things than that.

"What do you want to know, London?"

"About Karen."

"What is there to know? You want a biography? She came from Indiana because she wanted to be a success. A singer, an actress, a model, something. She wasn't too clear on just what. She tried, she flopped. She woke up one day knowing she wasn't going to make it. It happens."

I didn't say anything.

"So she could go back to Indiana or she could stay in the city. Only she couldn't go back to Indiana. You give in to enough men, you drink enough drinks and do enough things, then you can't go back to Indiana. What's left?"

She lit a cigarette. "Karen could have been a whore. But she wasn't. She never put a price tag on it. She spread it around, sure. Look, she was in New York and she was used to a certain kind of life and a certain kind of people, and she had to manage that life and those people into enough money to stay alive on, and she had one commodity to trade. She had sex. But she wasn't a whore." She paused. "There's a difference."

"All right."

"Well, dammit, what else do you want to know?"

"Who was she sleeping with besides Donahue?"

"She didn't say and I didn't ask. And she never kept a diary."

"She ever have men up here?"

"No."

"She talk much about Donahue?"

"No." She leaned over, stubbed out a cigarette. Her breasts loomed before my face like fruit. But it wasn't purposeful sexiness. She didn't play that way.

"I've got to get out of here," she said. "I don't feel like talking anymore."

"If you could just—"

"I couldn't just." She looked away. "In fifteen minutes I have to be uptown on the West Side. A guy there wants to take some pictures of me naked. He pays for my time, Mr. London. I'm a working girl."

"Are you working tonight?"

"Huh?"

"I asked if—"

"I heard you. What's the pitch?"

"I'd like to take you out to dinner."

"Why?"

"I'd like to talk to you."

"I'm not going to tell you anything I don't feel like telling you, London."

"I know that, Miss Gorski."

"And a dinner doesn't buy my company in bed, either. In case that's the idea."

"It isn't. I'm not all that hard up, Miss Gorski."

She was suddenly smiling. The smile softened her face all over and cut her age a good three years. Before she had been attractive. Now she was genuinely pretty.

"You give as good as you take."

"I try to."

"Is eight o'clock too late? I just got done with lunch a little while ago."

"Eight's fine," I said. "I'll see you."

I left. I walked the half block to my car and sat behind the wheel for a few seconds and thought about two girls I had met that day. Both blondes, one born that way, one self-made. One of them had poise, breeding and money, good diction and flawless bearing—and she added up to a tramp. The other *was* a tramp, in an amateurish sort of a way, and she talked tough and dropped an occasional final consonant. Yet she was the one who managed to retain a certain degree of dignity. Of the two, Ceil Gorski was more the lady.

At 3:30 I was up in Westchester County. The sky was bluer, the air fresher and the houses more costly. I pulled up in front of a $35,000 split-level, walked up a flagstone path and leaned on a doorbell.

The little boy who answered it had red hair, freckles and a chipped tooth. He was too cute to be snotty, but this didn't stop him.

He asked me who I was. I told him to get his father. He asked me why. I told him that if he didn't get his father I would twist his arm off. He wasn't sure whether or not to believe me, but I was obviously the first person who had ever talked to him this way. He took off in a hurry and a few seconds later Phil Abeles came to the door.

"Oh, London," he said. "Hello. Say, what did you tell the kid?"

"Nothing."

"Your face must have scared him." Abeles' eyes darted around. "You want to talk about what happened last night, I suppose."

"That's right."

"I'd just as soon talk somewhere else," he said. "Wait a minute, will you?"

I waited while he went to tell his wife that somebody from the office had driven up, that it was important, and that he'd be back in an hour. He came out and we went to my car.

"There's a quiet bar two blocks down and three over," he said, then added: "Let me check something. The way I've got it, you're a private detective working for Mark. Is that right?"

"Yes."

"Okay," he said. "I'd like to help the guy out. I don't know very much, but there are things I can talk about to you that I'd just as soon not tell the police. Nothing illegal. Just… Well, you can figure it out."

I could figure it out. That was the main reason why I had agreed to stay on the case for Donahue. People do not like to talk to the police if they can avoid it.

If Phil Abeles was going to talk at all about Karen Price, he would prefer me as a listening post to Lieutenant Jerry Gunther.

"Here's the place," he said. I pulled up next to the chosen bar, a log-cabin arrangement.

Abeles had J & B with water and I ordered a pony of Courvoisier.

"I told that homicide lieutenant I didn't know anything about the Price girl," he said. "That wasn't true."

"Go on."

He hesitated, but just a moment. "I didn't know she had any-thing going with Donahue," he said. "Nobody ever thought of Karen in one-man terms. She slept around."

"I gathered that."

"It's a funny thing," he said. "A girl, not exactly a whore but not convent-bred either, can tend to pass around in a certain group of men. Karen was like that. She went for ad men. I think at one time or another she was intimate with half of Madison Avenue."

Speaks well of the dead, I thought. "For anyone in particular?" I asked.

"It's hard to say. Probably for most of the fellows who were at the dinner last night. For Ray Powell—but that's nothing new; he's one of those bachelors who gets to everything in a skirt sooner or later. But for the married ones, too."

"For you?"

"That's a hell of a question."'

"Forget it. You already answered it."

He grinned sourly. "Yes—" he lapsed into flippant Madison Avenue talk "— the Price was right." He sipped his drink, then continued. "Not recently, and not often. Two or three times over two months ago. You won't blackmail me now, will you?"

"I don't play that way." I thought a minute. "Would Karen Price have tried a little subtle blackmail?"

"I don't think so. She played pretty fair."

"Was she the type to fall in love with somebody like Dona-hue?"

Abeles scratched his head. "The story I heard," he said. "Something to the effect that she was calling him, threatening him, trying to head off his marriage."

I nodded. "That's why he hired me."

"It doesn't make much sense."

"No?"

"No. It doesn't fit in with what I know about Karen. She wasn't the torch-bearer type. And she was hardly making a steady thing with Mark, either. I may not have known he was sleeping with her, but I knew damn well that a lot of other guys had been making with her lately."

"Could she have been shaking him down?"

He shrugged. "I told you," he said. "It doesn't sound like her. But who knows? She might have gotten into financial trouble. It happens. Perhaps she'd try to milk somebody for a little money." He pursed his lips. "But why should she blackmail Mark, for heaven's sake? If she blackmailed a bachelor he could always tell her to go to hell. You'd think she would work that on a married man, not a bachelor."

"I know."

He started to laugh then. "But not me," he said. "Believe me, London. She didn't blackmail me and I didn't kill her."

I got a list from him of all the men at the dinner. In addition to Donahue and myself, there had been eight men present, all of them from Darcy & Bates. Four—Abeles, Jack Harris, Harold Merriman and Joe Conn—were married. One—Ray Powell—was the bachelor and stud-about-town of the group, almost a compulsive Don Juan, according to Abeles. Another, Fred Klein, had a wife waiting out a residency requirement in Reno.

The remaining two wouldn't have much to do with girls like Karen Price. Lloyd Travers and Kenneth Bream were as queer as rectangular eggs.

I drove Abeles back to his house. Before I let him off he told me again not to waste time suspecting him.

"One thing you might remember," I said. "*Somebody* in that room shot Karen Price. Either Mark or one of the eight of you… I don't think it was Mark." I paused. "That means there's a murderer in your office, Abeles."

5

It was late enough in the day to call Lieutenant Gunther. I tried him at home first. His wife answered, told me he was at the station. I tried him there and caught him.

"Nice hours you work, Jerry."

"Well, I didn't have anything else on today. So I came on down. You know how it is… Say, I got news for you, Ed."

"About Donahue?"

"Yes. We let him go."

"He's clear?"

"No, not clear." Jerry grunted. "We could have held him but there was no point, Ed. He's not clear, not by a mile. But we ran a check on the Price kid and learned she's been sleeping with two parties—Democrats and Republicans. Practically everyone at the stag. So there's nothing that makes your boy look too much more suspicious than the others."

"I found out the same thing this afternoon."

"Ed, I wasn't too crazy about letting him get away. Donahue still looks like the killer from where I sit. He hired you because the girl was giving him trouble. She wasn't giving anybody else trouble. He looks like the closest thing to a suspect around."

"Then why release him?"

I could picture Jerry's shrug. "Well, there was pressure," he said. "The guy got himself an expensive lawyer and the lawyer was getting ready to pull a couple of strings. That's not all, of course. Donahue isn't a criminal type, Ed. He's not going to run far. We let him go figuring we won't have much trouble picking him up again."

"Maybe you won't have to."

"You get anything yet, Ed?"

"Not much," I said. "Just enough to figure out that every-thing's mixed up."

"I already knew that."

"Uh-huh. But the more I hunt around, the more loose ends I find. I'm glad you boys let my client loose. I'm going to see if I can get hold of him."

"Bye," Jerry said, clicking off.

I took time to get a pipe going, then dialed Mark Donahue's number. The phone rang eight times before I gave up. I decided he must be out on Long Island with Lynn Farwell. I was halfway through the complicated process of prying a number out of the information operator when I decided not to bother. Donahue had my number. He could reach me when he got the chance.

Then I closed my eyes, gritted my teeth and tried to think straight.

It wasn't easy. So far I had managed one little trick—I had succeeded in convincing myself that Donahue had not killed the girl. But this wasn't much cause for celebration. When you're working for someone, it's easy to get yourself to thinking that your client is on the side of the angels.

First of all, the girl. Karen Price. According to all and sundry, she was something of a tramp. According to her roommate she didn't put a price tag on it—but she didn't keep it under lock and key, either. She had wound up in bed with most of the het-erosexual ad men on Madison Avenue. Donahue, a member of this clan, had been sleeping with her.

This didn't mean she was in love with him, or carrying a flaming torch, or singing blues, or issuing dire threats con-cerning his upcoming marriage. According to everyone who knew Karen, there was no reason for her to give a whoop in hell whether he got married, turned queer, became an astronaut or joined the Foreign Legion.

But Donahue said he had received threatening calls from her. That left two possibilities. One: Donahue was lying. Two: Donahue was telling the truth.

If he was lying, why in hell had he hired me as a bodyguard? And if he had some other reason to want the girl dead, he wouldn't need me along for fun and games. Hell, if he hadn't gone through the business of hiring me, no one could have tagged him as the prime suspect in the shooting. He would just be another person at the bachelor dinner, another former play-mate of Karen's with no more motive to kill her than anyone else at the party.

I gave up the brainwork and concentrated on harmless if time-consuming games. I sat at my desk and drew up a list of the eight men who had been at the dinner. I listed the four married men, the Don Juan, the incipient divorce and, just for the sake of completion, Lloyd and Kenneth. I worked on my silly little list for over an hour, creating mythical motives for each man.

It made an interesting mental exercise, although it didn't seem to be of much value.

6

The Alhambra is a Syrian restaurant on West 27th Street, an Arabian oasis in a desert of Greek night clubs. Off the beaten track, it doesn't advertise, and the sign announcing its presence is almost invisible. You have to know the Alhambra is there in order to find it.

The owner and maitre d' is a little man whom the customers call Kamil. His name is Louis, his parents brought him to America before his eyes were open, and one of his brothers is a full professor at Columbia, but he likes to put on an act. When I brought Ceil Gorski into the place around 8:30, he smiled hugely at me and bowed halfway to the floor.

"*Salaam alekhim*," he said solemnly. "My pleasure, Mist' London."

"*Alekhim salaam*," I intoned, glancing over at Ceil while Louis showed us to a table.

Our waiter brought a bottle of very sweet white wine to go with the entree.

"I was bitchy before. I'm sorry about it."

"Forget it."

"Ed—"

I looked at her. She was worth looking at, in a pale green dress which she filled to perfe ction.

"You want to ask me some questions," she said, "don't you?"

"Well—"

"I don't mind, Ed."

I gave her a brief rundown on the way things seemed to shape up at that point.

"Let me try some names on you," I suggested. "Maybe you can tell me whether Karen mentioned them."

"You can try."

I ran through the eight jokers who had been at the stag. A few sounded vaguely familiar to her, but one of them, Ray Powell, turned out to be someone Ceil knew personally.

"A chaser," she said. "A very plush East Side apartment and an appetite for women that never lets up. He used to see Karen now and then, but there couldn't have been anything serious."

"You know him—very well?"

"Yes." She colored suddenly. She was not the sort you expected to blush. "If you mean intimately, no. He asked often enough. I wasn't interested." She lowered her eyes. "I don't sleep around that much," she said. "Karen—well, she came to New York with stars in her eyes, and when the stars dimmed and died, she went a little crazy, I suppose. I wasn't that ambitious and didn't fall as hard. I have some fairly far-out ways of earning a living, Ed, but most nights I sleep alone."

She was one hell of a girl. She was hard and soft, a cynic and a romantic at the same time. She hadn't gone to college, hadn't finished high school, but somewhere along the way she had acquired a veneer of sophistication that reflected more concrete knowledge than a diploma.

"Poor Karen," she said. "Poor Karen."

I didn't say anything. She sat somberly for a moment, then tossed her head so that her bleached blonde mane rippled like a wheat field in the wind. "I'm getting morbid as hell," she said. "You'd better take me home, Ed."

We climbed three flights of stairs. I stood next to her while she rummaged through her purse. She came up with a key and turned to face me before opening the door. "Ed," she said softly, "if I asked you, would you just come in for a few drinks? Could it be that much of an invitation and no more?"

"Yes."

"I hate to sound like—"

"I understand."

We went inside. She turned on lamps in the living room and we sat on the couch.

She started talking about the modeling session she'd gone through that afternoon. "The money was good," she said, "but I had to work for it. He took three or four rolls of film. Slightly advanced cheesecake, Ed. Nudes, underwear stuff. He'll print the best pictures and they'll wind up for sale in the dirty little stores on 42nd Street."

"With the face retouched?"

She laughed. "He won't bother. Nobody's going to look at the face, Ed."

"I would."

"Would you?"

"Yes."

"And not the body?"

"That too."

She looked at me for a long moment. There was something electric in the air. I could feel the sweet animal heat of her. She was right next to me. I could reach out and touch her, could take her in my arms and press her close. The bedroom wasn't far away. And she would be good, very good.

Two drinks later, I got up and walked to the door. She followed me. I stopped at the doorway, started to say something, changed my mind. We said goodnight and I started down the stairs.

If she had been just any girl—actress, secretary, college girl or waitress—then it would have ended differently. It would have ended in her bedroom, in warmth and hunger and fury. But she was not just any girl. She was a halfway tramp, a little tarnished, a little soiled, a little battered around the edges. And so I could not make that pass at her, could not maneuver from couch to bed.

I didn't want to go back to my apartment. It would be lonely there. I drove to a Third Avenue bar where they pour good drinks.

Somewhere between two and three I left the bar and looked around for the Chevy. By the time I found it I decided to leave it there and take a cab. I had had too little sleep the night before and too much to drink this night, and things were beginning to go a little out of focus. The way I felt, they looked better that way. But I didn't much feel like bouncing the car off a telephone pole or gunning down some equally stoned pedestrian. I flagged a cab and left the driving to him.

He had to tell me three times that we were in front of my building before it got through to me. I shook myself awake, paid him, and wended my way into the brownstone and up a flight of stairs.

Then I blinked a few times.

There was something on my doormat, something that hadn't been there when I left.

It was blonde, well-bred and glassy-eyed. It had an empty wine bottle in one hand and its mouth was smiling lustily. It got to its feet and swayed there, then pitched forward slightly. I caught it and it burrowed its head against my chest.

"You keep late hours," it said.

It was very soft and very warm. It rubbed its hips against me and purred like a kitten. I growled like a randy old tomcat.

"I've been waiting for you," it said. "I've been wanting to go to bed. Take me to bed, Ed London."

Its name, in case you haven't guessed, was Lynn Farwell.

We were a pair of iron filings and my bed was a magnet. I opened the door and we hurried inside. I closed the door and slid the bolt. We moved quickly through the living room and along a hall to the bedroom. Along the way we discarded clothing.

She left her skirt on my couch, her sweater on one of my leather chairs. Her bra and slip and shoes landed in various spots on the hall floor. In the bedroom she got rid of her stockings and garter belt and panties. She was naked and beautiful and hungry...and there was no time to waste on words.

Her body welcomed me. Her breasts, firm little cones of happiness, quivered against me. Her thighs enveloped me in the lust-heat of desire. Her face twisted in a blind agony of need.

We were both pretty well stoned. This didn't matter. We could never have done better sober. There was a beginning, bittersweet and almost painful. There was a middle, fast and furious, a scherzo movement in a symphony of fire. And there was an ending, gasping, spent, two bodies washed up on a lonely barren beach.

At the end she used words that girls are not supposed to learn in the schools she had attended. She screamed them out in a frenzy of completion, a song of obscenity offered as a coda.

And afterward, when the rhythm was gone and only the glow remained, she talked. "I needed that," she told me. "Needed it badly. But you could tell that, couldn't you?"

"Yes."

"You're good, Ed." She caressed me. "Very good."

"Sure. I win blue ribbons."

"Was I good?"

I told her she was fine.

"Mmmmm," she said.

7

I rolled out of bed just as the noon whistles started going off all over town. Lynn was gone. I listened to bells from a nearby church ring twelve times; then I showered, shaved and swallowed aspirin. Lynn had left. Living proof of indiscretions makes bad company on the morning after.

I caught a cab, and the driver and I prowled Third Avenue for my car. It was still there. I drove it back to the garage and tucked it away. Then I called Donahue, but hung up before the phone had a chance to ring. Not that I expected to reach him anyway, since calling him on the phone didn't seem to produce much in the way of concrete results. But I didn't feel like talking to him just then.

A few hours ago I had been busy coupling with his bride-to-be. It seemed an unlikely prelude to a conversation.

Darcy & Bates wasn't really on Madison Avenue. It was around the corner on 48th Street, a suite of offices on the fourteenth floor of a twenty-two story building. I got out of the elevator and stood before a reception desk.

"Phil Abeles," I said.

"May I ask your name?"

"Go right ahead." I smiled. She looked unhappy. "Ed London," I finally said. She smiled gratefully and pressed one of twenty buttons and spoke softly into a tube.

"If you'll have a seat, Mr. London," she said.

I didn't have a seat. I stood instead and loaded up a pipe. I finished lighting it as Abeles emerged from an office and came over to meet me. He motioned for me to follow him. We went into his air-cooled office and he closed the door.

"What's up, Ed?"

"I'm not sure," I said. "I want some help." I drew on the pipe. "I'll need a private office for an hour or two," I told him. "And I want to see all of the men who were at Mark Donahue's bachelor dinner. One at a time."

"All of us?" He grinned. "Even Lloyd and Kenneth?"

"I suppose we can pass them for the time being. Just you and the other five then. Can you arrange it?"

He nodded with a fair amount of enthusiasm. "You can use

this office," he said. "And everybody's around today, so you won't have any trouble on that score. Who do you want to see first?"

"I might as well start with you, Phil."

I talked with him for ten minutes. But I had already pumped him dry the day before. Still, he gave me a little information on some of the others I would be seeing. Before, I had tried to ask him about his own relationship with Karen Price. Although that tack had been fairly effective, it didn't look like the best way to come up with something concrete. Instead, I asked him about the other men. If I worked on all of them that way, I just might turn up an answer or two.

Abeles more or less crossed Fred Klein off the suspect list, if nothing else. Klein, whose wife was in Reno, had tentatively made the coulda-dunnit sheet on the chance that Karen was threatening to give his wife information that could boost her alimony, or something of the sort. Abeles knocked the theory to pieces with the information that Klein's wife had money of her own, that she wasn't looking for alimony, and that a pair of expensive lawyers had already worked out all the details of the divorce agreement.

I asked Phil Abeles which of the married men he knew definitely had contact at one time or another with Karen Price. This was the sort of information a man is supposed to keep to himself, but the mores of Madison Avenue tend to foster subtle back-stabbing. Abeles told me he knew for certain that Karen had been intimate with Harold Merriman, and he was almost sure about Joe Conn as well.

After Abeles left, I knocked the dottel out of my pipe and filled it again. I lit it, and as I shook out the match, I looked up at Harold Merriman.

A pudgy man with a bald spot and bushy eyebrows, forty or forty-five, somewhat older than the rest of the crew. He sat down across the desk from me and narrowed his eyes. "Phil said you wanted to see me," he said. "What's the trouble?"

"Just routine." I smiled. "I need a little information. You knew Karen Price before the shooting, didn't you?"

"Well, I knew who she was."

Sure, I thought. But I let it pass and played him the way I had planned. I asked him who in the office had had anything to do with the dead girl. He hemmed and hawed a little, then told me that Phil Abeles had taken her out for dinner once or twice and that Jack Harris was supposed to have had her along on a business trip to Miami one weekend. Strictly in a secretarial capacity, no doubt.

"And you?"

"Oh, no," Merriman said. "I'd met her, of course, but that was as far as it went."

"Really?"

The hesitation was admission enough. "Listen," he stammered, "all right, I...saw her a few times. It was nothing serious and it wasn't very recent. London—"

I waited.

"Keep it a secret, will you?" He forced a grin. "Write it off as a symptom of the foolish forties. She was available and I was ready to play around a little. I'd just as soon it didn't get out. Nobody around here knows, and I'd like to keep it that way." He hesitated again. "My wife knows. I was so damn ashamed of myself that I told her. But I wouldn't want the boys in the office to know."

I didn't tell him that they already knew, and that they had passed the information on to me.

Ray Powell came in grinning. He was a bachelor, and this made a difference. "Hello, London," he said. "I made it with the girl, if that's what you want to know."

"I heard rumors."

"I don't keep secrets," he said. He sprawled in the chair across from me and crossed one leg over the other. It was a relief to talk to someone other than a reticent, guilt-ridden adulterer.

He certainly looked like a Don Juan. He was twenty-eight, tall, dark and handsome, with wavy black hair and piercing brown eyes. A little prettier and he might have passed for a gigolo. But there was a slight hardness about his features that prevented this.

"You're working for Mark," he said.

"That's right."

He sighed. "Well, I'd like to see him wind up innocent, but from where I sit, it's hard to see it that way. He's a funny guy, London. He wants to have his cake and eat it, too. He wanted a marriage and he wanted a playmate. With the girl he was marrying, you wouldn't think he'd worry about playing around. Ever meet Lynn?"

"I've met her."

"Then you know what I mean."

I nodded. "Was she one of your conquests?"

"Lynn?" He laughed easily. "Not that girl. She's the pure type, London. The one-man woman. Mark found himself a sweet girl there. Why he bothered with Karen is beyond me."

I switched the subject to the married men in the office. With Powell, I didn't try to find out which of them had been intimate with Karen Price, since it seemed fairly obvious they all had. Instead I tried to ascertain which of them could be in trouble as a result of an affair with the girl.

I learned a few things. Jack Harris was immune to blackmail— his wife knew he cheated on her regularly and had schooled herself to ignore such indiscretions just as long as he returned to her after each rough passage through the turbulent waters of adultery.

Harold Merriman was sufficiently well-off financially so that he could pay a blackmailer indefinitely rather than quiet her by murder; besides, Merriman had already told me that his wife knew, and I was more or less prepared to believe him.

Both Abeles and Joe Conn were possibilities. Conn looked best of all. He wasn't doing very well in advertising but he could hold his job indefinitely—he had married a girl whose family ran one of Darcy & Bates' major accounts. Conn had no money of his own, and no talent to hold a job if his wife wised up and left him.

Of course, there was always the question of how valid Ray Powell's impressions were. *Lynn? She's the pure type. The one-man woman.*

That didn't sound much like the drunken blonde who had turned up on my doorstep the night before.

Jack Harris revealed nothing new, merely reinforced what I had managed to pick up elsewhere along the line. I talked to him for fifteen minutes or so. He left, and Joe Conn came into the room.

He wasn't happy. "They said you wanted to see me," he muttered. "We'll have to make it short, London. I've got a pile of work this afternoon and my nerves are jumping all over the place as it is."

The part about the nerves was something he didn't have to tell me. He didn't sit still, just paced back and forth like a lion in a cage before chow time.

I could play it slow and easy or fast and hard, looking to shock and jar. If he was the one who killed her, his nervousness now gave me an edge. I decided to press it.

I got up, walked over to Conn. A short stocky man, crew cut, no tie. "When did you start sleeping with Karen?" I snapped.

He spun around wide-eyed. "You're crazy!"

"Don't play games," I told him. "The whole office knows you were bedding her."

I watched him. His hands curled into fists at his sides. His eyes narrowed and his nostrils flared.

"What is this, London?"

"Your wife doesn't know about Karen, does she?"

"Damn you." He moved toward me. "How much, you bastard? A private detective," he snickered. "Sure you are. You're a damn blackmailer, London. How much?"

"Just how much did Karen ask for?" I said. "Enough to make you kill her?"

He answered with a left hook that managed to find the point of my chin and send me crashing back against the wall. There was a split second of blackness. Then he was coming at me again, fists ready, and I spun aside, ducked and planted a fist of my own in his gut. He grunted and threw a right at me. I took it on the shoulder and tried his belly again. It was softer this time. He wheezed and folded up. I hit him in the face and just managed to pull the punch at the last minute. It didn't knock him out—only spilled him on the seat of his tweed pants.

"You've got a good punch, London."

"So do you," I said. My jaw still ached.

"You ever do any boxing?"

"No."

"I did," he said. "In the Navy. I still try to keep in shape. If I hadn't been so angry I'd have taken you."

"Maybe."

"But I got mad," he said. "Irish temper, I guess. Are you trying to shake me down?"

"No."

"You don't honestly think I killed Karen, do you?"

"Did you?"

"God, no."

I didn't say anything.

"You think I killed her," he said hollowly. "You must be insane. I'm no killer, London."

"Of course. You're a meek little man."

"You mean just now? I lost my temper."

"Sure."

"Oh, hell," he said. "I never killed her. You got me mad. I don't like shakedowns and I don't like being called a murderer. That's all, damn you."

I called Jerry Gunther from a pay phone in the lobby. "Two things," I told the lieutenant. "First I think I've got a hotter prospect for you than Donahue. A man named Joe Conn, one of the boys at the stag. I tried shaking him up a little and he cracked wide open, tried to beat my brains in. He's got a good motive, too."

"Ed, listen—"

"That's the first thing," I said. "The other is that I've been trying to get in touch with my client for the past too-many hours and can't reach him. Did you have him picked up again?"

There was a long pause. All at once the air in the phone booth felt much too close. Something was wrong.

"I saw Donahue half an hour ago," Jerry said. "I'm afraid he killed that girl, Ed."

"He confessed?" I couldn't believe it.

"He confessed…in a way."

"I don't get it."

A short sigh. "It happened yesterday," Jerry said. "I can't give you the time until we get the medical examiner's report, but the guess is that it was just after we let him go. He sat down at his typewriter and dashed off a three-line confession. Then he stuck a gun in his mouth and made a mess. The lab boys are still there trying to scrape his brains off the ceiling. Ed?"

"What?"

"You didn't say anything…I didn't know if you were still on the line. Look, everybody guesses wrong some of the time."

"This was more than a guess. I was sure."

"Well, listen, I'm on my way to Donahue's place again. If you want to take a run over there you can have a look for yourself. I don't know what good it's going to do—"

"I'll meet you there," I said.

8

The lab crew left shortly after we arrived. "Just a formality for the inquest," Jerry Gunther said. "That's all."

"You're sure it's a suicide, then?"

"Stop dreaming, Ed. What else?"

What else? All that was left in the world of Mark Donahue was sprawled in a chair at a desk. There was a typewriter in front of him and a gun on the floor beside him. The gun was just where it would have dropped after a suicide shot of that nature. There were no little inconsistencies.

The suicide note in the typewriter was slightly incoherent. It read: *It has to end now. I can't help what I did but there is no way out anymore. God forgive me and God help me. I am sorry.*

"You can go if you want, Ed. I'll stick around until they send a truck for the body. But—"

"Run over the timetable, will you?"

"From when to when?"

"From when you released him to when he died."

Jerry shrugged. "Why? You can't read it any way but suicide, can you?"

"I don't know. Give me a rundown."

"Let's see," he said. "You called around five, right?"

"Around then. Five or five-thirty."

"We let him go around three. There's your timetable, Ed. We let him out around three, he came back here, thought about things for a while, then wrote that note and killed himself. That checks with the rough estimate we've got of the time of death. You narrow it down—you did call him after I spoke to you, didn't you?"

"Yes. No answer."

"He must have been dead by that time; probably killed himself within an hour after he got here."

"How did he seem when you released him?"

"Happy to be out, I thought at the time. But he didn't show much emotion one way or the other. You know how it is with a person who's getting ready to knock himself off. All the problems and emotions are kept bottled up inside."

I went over to a window and looked out at Horatio Street. It was the most obvious suicide in the world, but I couldn't swallow it. Call it a hunch, a stubborn refusal to accept the fact that my client had managed to fool me. Whatever it was, I didn't believe the suicide theory. It just didn't sit right.

"I don't like it," I said. "I don't think he killed himself."

"You're wrong, Ed."

"Am I?" I went to Donahue's liquor cabinet and filled two glasses with cognac.

"I know nothing ever looked more like suicide," I admitted. "But the motives are still as messy as ever. Look at what we've got here. We have a man who hired me to protect him from his former mistress—and as soon as he did, he only managed to call attention to the fact that he was involved with her. He received threatening phone calls from her. She didn't want him married. But her best friend swears that the Price girl didn't give a damn about Donahue, that he was only another man in her collection."

"Look, Ed—"

"Let me finish. We can suppose for a minute that he was lying for reasons of his own that don't make much sense, that he had some crazy reason for calling me in on things before he knocked off the girl. Maybe he thought that would alibi him—"

"That's just what I was going to say," Jerry interjected.

"I thought of it. It doesn't make a hell of a lot of sense, but it's possible, I guess. Still, where in hell is his motive? Not blackmail. She wasn't the blackmailing type to begin with, as far as I can see. But there's more to it than that. Lynn Farwell wouldn't care who Mark slept with before they were married. Or after, for that matter. It wasn't a love match. She wanted a respectable husband and he wanted a rich wife, and they both figured to get what they wanted. Love wasn't part of it."

"Maybe he wasn't respectable," Jerry said. "Maybe Karen knew something he didn't want known. There's plenty of room here for a hidden motive, Ed."

"Maybe. Still I wish you'd keep the case open, Jerry."

"You know I won't."

"You'll write it off as suicide and close the file?"

"I have to. All the evidence points that way. Murder and then suicide, with Donahue tagged for killing the Price girl and then killing himself."

"I guess it makes your bookkeeping easier."

"You know better than that, Ed." He almost sounded hurt. "If I could see it any other way I'd keep on it. I can't. As far as we're concerned it's a closed book."

I walked over to the window again. "I'm going to stay with it," I said.

"Without a client?"

"Without a client."

A maid answered the phone in the Farwell home. I asked to speak to Lynn.

"Miss Farwell's not home," she said. "Who's calling, please?"

I gave her my name.

"Oh, yes, Mr. London. Miss Farwell left a message for you to call her at—" I took down a number with a Regency exchange, thanked her and hung up.

I was tired, unhappy and confused. I didn't want the role of bearer of evil tidings. I wished now that I had let Jerry tell her himself. I was in my apartment, it was a hot day for the time of the year, and my air conditioner wasn't working right. I dialed the number the maid had given me. A girl answered, not Lynn. I asked to speak to Miss Farwell.

She came on the line almost immediately. "Ed?"

"Yes. I—"

"I wondered if you'd call. I hope I wasn't horrid last night. I was very drunk."

"You were all right."

"Just all right?" I didn't say anything. She giggled softly and whispered, "I had a good time, Ed. Thank you for a lovely evening."

"Lynn—"

"Is something the matter?"

I've never been good at breaking news. I took a deep breath and blurted out, "Mark is dead. I just came from his apartment. The police think he killed himself."

Silence.

"Can I meet you somewhere, Lynn? I'd like to talk to you."

More silence. Then, when she did speak, her voice was flat as week-old beer. "Are you at your apartment?"

"Yes."

"Stay there. I'll be right over. I'll take a cab."

The line went dead.

9

While I waited for Lynn I thought about Joe Conn. If one person murdered both Karen Price and Mark Donahue, Conn seemed the logical suspect. Karen was blackmailing him, I reasoned, holding him up for hush money that he had to pay if he wanted to keep wife and job. He found out Karen was going to be at the stag, jumping out of the cake, and he took a gun along and shot her.

Then Mark got arrested and Conn felt safe. Just when he was most pleased with himself, the police released Mark. Conn started to worry. If the case dragged out he was in trouble. Even if they didn't get to him, a lengthy investigation would turn up the fact that he had been sleeping with Karen. And he had to keep that fact hidden.

So he went to Donahue's apartment with another gun. He hit Mark over the head, propped him up in the chair, shot him through the mouth and replaced his own prints with Mark's. Then he dashed off a quick suicide note and got out of there. The blow on the head wouldn't show, if that was how he did it. Not after the bullet did things to Mark's skull.

But then why in hell did Conn throw a fit at the ad agency when I tried to ruffle him? It didn't make sense. If he had killed Mark on Sunday afternoon, he would know that it would be only a matter of time until the body was found and the case closed. He wouldn't blow up if I called him a murderer, not when he had already taken so much trouble to cover his tracks.

Unless he was being subtle, anticipating my whole line of reasoning. And when you start taking a suspect's possible sub-tlety into consideration, you find yourself on a treadmill marked confusion. All at once the possibilities become endless.

I got off the treadmill, though. The doorbell rang and Lynn Farwell stepped into my apartment for the third time in two days. And it occurred to me, suddenly, just how different each of those three visits had been.

This one was slightly weird. She walked slowly to the same leather chair in which she had curled up Saturday morning. She did not wax kittenish this time.

"I don't feel a thing," she said.

"Shock."

"No," she admitted. "I don't even feel shock, Ed. I just don't feel a thing.

"I wasn't in love with him," she said. "You knew that, of course."

"I gathered as much."

"It wasn't a well-kept secret, was it? I told you that much before I told you my name, almost. Of course I was on the make for you at the time. That may have had something to do with it."

She looked at her drink but didn't touch it. Slowly, softly she said, "After the first death there is no other."

There was a minute of silence. Just as I was about to prompt her into speaking, she repeated, "After the first death there is no other." She sighed. "When one death affects you completely, then the deaths that come after it don't have their full effect. Do you follow me?"

I nodded. "When did it happen?" I asked.

"Four years ago. I was in college then."

"A boy?"

"Yes."

She looked at her drink, then drained it.

"I was nineteen then. Pure and innocent. A popular girl who dated all the best boys and had a fine time. Then I met him. Ray Powell introduced us. You probably met Ray. He worked in the same office as Mark."

I nodded. That explained one contradiction—Ray's referring to Lynn as the pure type, the one-man woman. When he had known her, the shoe fit. Since then she had outgrown it.

"I started going out with John and all at once I was in love. I had never been in love before. I've never been in love since. It was something." For a shadow of an instant a smile crossed her face, then disappeared. "I can't honestly remember what it was like. Being in love, that is. I'm not the same person. That girl could love; I can't.

"He was going to pick me up and something went wrong with his car. The steering wheel or something like that. He was going around a turn and the wheels wouldn't straighten out and—

"I changed after that. At first I just hurt. All over. And then the callus formed, the emotional callus to keep me from going crazy, I suppose." She picked up a cigarette and puffed on it nervously then stubbed it out. "You know what bothered me most? We never slept together. We were going to wait until we were married. See what a corny little girl I was?

"But I changed, Ed. I thought that at least I could have given him that much before he died. And I thought about that, and maybe brooded about it, and something happened inside me." She almost smiled. "I'm afraid I became a little bit of a tramp, Ed. Not just now and then, like last night. A tramp.

I went to Ray Powell and lost my virginity, and then I made myself a one-woman welcoming committee for visiting Yale boys."

Her face filled up with memories. "I'm not that bad anymore. And I don't honestly feel John's death either, to be truthful. It happened a long time ago, and to a different girl."

"I don't think Mark Donahue killed himself," I said, "or the girl. I think he was framed and then murdered."

"It doesn't matter."

"Doesn't it?"

"No," she said, sadly, vacantly. "It should, I know. But it doesn't, Ed." She stood up. "Do you know why I really wanted to come here?"

"To talk."

"Yes. I've learned to pretend, you see. And I intend to pretend, too. I'll be the very shocked and saddened Miss Farwell now. That's the role I have to play." Another too-brief smile. "But I don't have to play that role with you, Ed. I wanted to say what I felt if only to one person. Or what I didn't feel." She rose to leave.

"And now I'll wear imitation widow's weeds for a while, and then I'll find some other bright young man to marry. Goodbye, Ed London."

I almost forgot about the date with Ceil. I'd made it the night before instead of the pass I would have preferred to make. When I got there, she said she was tired and hot and didn't feel like dressing.

"The Britannia is right down the block," she said. "And I can go there like this."

She was wearing slacks and a man's shirt. She didn't look mannish, though. That would have been slightly impossible.

We walked down the block to a hole in the wall with a sign that said, appropriately, FISH AND CHIPS. There were half a dozen small tables in a room decorated with travel posters of Trafalgar Square and Buckingham Palace and every major British tourist attraction with the possible exception of Diana Dors. We sat at a small table and ordered fish and chips and bottles of Guinness.

I said, "Donahue's dead."

"I know. I heard it on the radio."

"What did they say?"

"Suicide. He confessed to the murder and shot himself. Isn't that what happened?"

"I don't think so." I signaled the waiter for two more bottles of Guinness.

"It's possible that someone—probably Conn—killed Donahue," I added. "The door to his apartment was locked when the police got there, but it's one of those spring locks. The inside bolt wasn't turned. Conn could have gone there as soon as he learned Mark was released, then shot him and locked the door as he left."

"How could he know Mark was released?"

"A phone call to Police Headquarters, or a call to Mark. That's no problem."

"How about the time? Maybe Conn has an alibi."

"I'm going to check that tomorrow," I said. "That's why I would have liked to see Jerry Gunther keep the file open on the case. Then he could have questioned Conn. The guy threw punches at me once already. I don't know if I can take him a second time."

She grinned. Then her face sobered. "Are you sure it was Conn? You said Abeles had the same motive."

"He's also got an alibi."

"A good one?"

"Damn good. *I'm* his alibi. I was with him in Scarsdale that afternoon, and I called Donahue's apartment as soon as I got back to town, and by that time Donahue was dead. Phil Abeles would have needed a jet plane to pull it off. Besides, I can't see him as the killer."

"And you can see Conn?"

"That's the trouble," I said. "I can't. Not really."

We drank up. I paid our check and we left. We walked a block to Washington Square and sat on a bench. I started to smoke my pipe when I heard a sharp intake of breath and turned to stare at Ceil.

"Oh," she said. "I just had a grisly idea."

"What?"

"It's silly. Like an Alfred Hitchcock television show. I thought maybe Karen really did make those phone calls to him, not because she was jealous but just to tease him, thinking what a gag it would be when she popped out of the cake at his bachelor dinner. And then the gag backfires and he shoots her because he's scared she wants to kill him." She laughed. "I've got a cute imagination," she said. "But I'm not much of a help, am I?"

I didn't answer her. My mind was off on a limb somewhere. I closed my eyes and saw the waiters wheeling the cake out toward the center of the room. Stripper music playing on a phonograph. A girl bursting from the cake, nude and lovely. A wide smile on her face—

"Ed, what's the matter?"

Most of the time problems are solved by simple trial and error, a lot of legwork that pays off finally. Other times all the legwork in the world falls flat, and it's like a jigsaw puzzle where you suddenly catch the necessary piece and all the others leap into place. This was one of those times.

"You're a genius!" I told Ceil.

"You don't mean it happened that way? I—"

"Oh, no. Of course not. Donahue didn't kill Karen—" I stood.

"Hey, where are you going?" Ceil asked.

"Gotta run," I said. "Can't even walk you home. Tomorrow," I said. "We'll have dinner, okay?"

I didn't hear her answer. I didn't wait for it. I raced across the park and jumped into the nearest cab.

I called Lynn Farwell from my apartment. She was back in her North Shore home, and life had returned to her voice. "I didn't expect to hear from you," she said. "I suppose you're interested in my body, Ed. It wouldn't be decent so soon after Mark's death, you know. But you may be able to persuade me—"

"Not your body," I said. "Your memory. Can you talk now? Without being overheard?"

She giggled lewdly. "If I couldn't, I wouldn't have said what I did. Go ahead, Mr. Detective."

I asked questions. She gave me answers. They were the ones I wanted to hear.

I strapped on a shoulder holster and jammed a gun into it.

10

The door to Powell's apartment was locked. I rang the bell once. No one answered. I waited a few minutes, then took out my pen knife and went to work on the lock. Like the locks in all decent buildings in New York, this was one of the burglar-proof models. And, like just 99 percent of them, it wasn't burglar-proof. It took half a minute to open.

I turned the knob. Then I eased the gun from my shoulder

holster and shoved the door open. I didn't need the gun just then. The room was empty.

But the apartment wasn't. I heard noises from another room, people-noises, sex-noises. A man's voice and a girl's voice. The man was saying he heard somebody in the living room. The girl was telling him he was crazy. He said he would check. Then there were footsteps, and he came through the doorway, and I pointed the gun at him.

I said, "Stay right there, Powell."

He looked a little ridiculous. He was wearing a bathrobe, his feet were bare, and it was fairly obvious that he had been interrupted somewhere in the middle of his favorite pastime. I kept the gun on him and watched his eyes. He was good—damned good. The eyes showed fear, outrage, surprise. Nothing else. Not the look of a man in a trap.

"If this is some kind of a joke—"

"It's no joke."

"Then what the hell is it?"

"The end of the line," I said. "You made a hell of a try. You almost got away with it."

"I don't know what you're driving at, London. But—"

"I think you do."

She picked that moment to wander into the room. She was a redhead with her hair messed. One of the buttons on her blouse was buttoned wrong. She walked into the room, wondering aloud what the interruption was about, and then she saw the gun and her mouth made a little O.

She said, "Maybe I should of stood in the other room."

"Maybe you should go home," I snapped.

"Oh," she said. "Yes, that's a very good idea." She moved to her left and sort of backed around me, as if she wanted to keep as much distance as possible between her well-constructed body and the gun in my hand. "I think you're right," she said. "I think I should go home… And you don't have to worry about me."

"Good."

"I should tell you I have no memory at all," she said. "I never came here, never met you, never saw your face, and I cannot possibly remember what you look like. It is terrible, my memory."

"Good," I said.

"Living I like very much better than remembering. Goodbye, Mr. Nobody."

The door slammed, and Ray Powell and I were alone. He glared at me.

"What in hell do you want, exactly?"

"To talk to you."

"You need a gun for that?"

"Probably."

He grinned disarmingly. "Guns make me nervous."

"They never did before. You've got a knack for getting hold of unregistered guns, Powell. Is there another one in the bedroom?"

"I don't get it," he said. He scratched his head. "You must mean something, London. Spit it out."

"Don't play games."

"I—"

"Cut it," I said. "You killed Karen Price. You knew she was going to do the cake bit because you were the one who put the idea in Phil Abeles' head."

"Did he tell you that?"

"He's forgotten. But he'll remember with a little prompting. You set her up and then you killed her and tossed the gun on the floor. You figured the police would arrest Donahue, and you were right. But you didn't think they would let him go. When they did, you went to his place with another gun. He let you in. You shot him, made it look like suicide, and let the one death cover the other."

He shook his head in wonder. "You really believe this?"

"I know it."

"I suppose I had a motive," he said musingly. "What, pray tell, did I have against the girl? She was good in bed, you know. I make it a rule never to kill a good bed partner if I can help it." He grinned. "So why did I kill her?"

"You didn't have a thing against her," I said.

"My point exactly. I—"

"You killed her to frame Donahue," I added. "You got to Karen Price while the bachelor dinner was still in the planning stage. You hired her to make a series of calls to Donahue, jealous calls threatening to kill him or otherwise foul up his wedding. It was going to be a big joke—she would scare him silly; and then for a capper she would pop out of the cake as naked as the truth and tell him she was just pulling his leg.

"But you topped the gag. She popped out of the cake covered with a smile and you put a bullet in her and left Donahue looking like the killer. Then, when you thought he was getting off the hook, you killed him. Not to cover the first murder— you felt safe enough on that score…because you really didn't have a reason to kill the girl herself. You killed Donahue because he was the one you wanted dead all along."

Powell was still grinning. Only not so self-assuredly now. In the beginning, he hadn't been aware of how much I knew. Now he was learning and it wasn't making him happy.

"I'll play your game," he said. "I killed Karen, even though I didn't have any reason. Now why did I kill Mark? Did I have a reason for that one?"

"Sure."

"What?"

"For the same reason you hired Karen to bother Donahue," I said. "Maybe a psychiatrist could explain it better. He'd call it transference."

"Go on."

"You wanted Mark Donahue dead because he was going to marry Lynn Farwell. And you don't want anybody to marry Lynn Farwell. Powell, you'd kill anybody who tried."

"Keep talking," he said.

"How am I doing so far?"

"Oh, you're brilliant, London. I suppose I'm in love with Lynn?"

"In a way."

"That's why I've never asked her to marry me. And why I bed down anything else that gets close enough to jump."

"That's right."

"You're out of your mind, London."

"No," I said. "But you are." I took a breath. "You've been in love with Lynn for a long time. Four years, anyway. It's no normal love, Powell, because you're not a normal person. Lynn's part of a fixation of yours. She's sweet and pure and unattainable in your mind. You don't want to possess her completely because that would destroy the illusion. Instead you compensate by proving your virility with any available girl. But you can't let Lynn marry someone else. That would take her away from you. You don't want to have her—except for an occasional evening, maybe—but you won't let anyone else have her."

He was tottering on the edge now…trying to take a step toward me and then backing off. I had to push him over that edge. If he cracked, then he would crack wide open. If he held himself together he might wriggle free. I knew damn well he was guilty, but there wasn't enough evidence to present to a jury. I had to make him crack.

"First I'm a double murderer," Powell said. "Now I'm a

mental case. I don't deny that I like Lynn. She's a sweet, clean, decent girl. But that's as far as it goes."

"Is it?"

"Yes."

"Donahue's the second man who almost married her. The first one was four years ago. Remember John? You introduced the two of them. That was a mistake, wasn't it?"

"He wouldn't have been good for her. But it didn't matter. I suppose you know he died in a car accident."

"In a car, yes. Not an accident. You gimmicked the steering wheel. Then you let him kill himself. You got away clean with that one, Powell."

I hadn't cracked him yet. I was close, but he was still able to compose himself.

"It was an accident," he exclaimed. "Besides, it happened a long time ago. I'm surprised you even bother mentioning it."

I ignored his words. "The death shook Lynn up a lot," I said. "It must have been tough for you to preserve your image of her. The sweet and innocent thing turned into a round-heeled little nymph for a while."

"That's a damned lie."

"It is like hell. And about that time you managed to have your cake and eat it, too. You kept on thinking of her as the unattainable ideal. But that didn't stop you from taking her virginity, did it? You ruined her, Powell!"

He was getting closer to the borderline. His face was white and his hands were hard little fists. The muscles in his neck were drum-tight.

"I never touched her!"

"Liar!" I was shouting now. "You ruined that girl, Powell!"

"Damn you, I never touched her! Nobody did, damn you! She's still a virgin! She's still a virgin!"

I took a breath. "The hell she is," I yelled. "I had her last night, Powell. She came to my room all hot to trot and I bedded her until she couldn't see straight."

His eyes were wild.

"Did you hear me, Powell? I had *your girl* last night. I had Lynn, Powell!"

And that cracked him.

He charged me like a wild man, his whole body coordinated in the spring. I stepped back, swung aside. He tried to turn and come toward me but his momentum kept him from pulling it off. By the time he got back on the right track, my hand had gone up and come down. The barrel of the gun caught him just behind the left ear. He took two more little steps, carried along by the sheer force of his rush. Then he folded up and went out like an ebbing tide.

He wasn't out long. By the time Jerry Gunther got there, flanked by a pair of uniformed cops, Powell was babbling away a mile a minute, spending half the time confessing to the three murders and the other half telling anyone who would listen that Lynn Farwell was a saint.

They started to put handcuffs on him. Then they changed their minds and bundled him up in a straitjacket.

I I

"I guess I missed my calling," Ceil said. "I should have been a detective. I probably would have flopped there, too, but the end might have been different. We all know what girls become when they don't make it as actresses. What do lousy detectives turn to?"

"Cognac," I said. "Pass the bottle."

She passed and I poured. We were in her apartment on Sullivan Street. It was Tuesday night, Ray Powell had long since finished confessing, and Ceil Gorski had just proved to me that she could cook a good meal.

"You figured it out beautifully," she said. "But do I get an assist on the play?"

"Easily." I tucked tobacco into my pipe, lit up. "You managed to get my mind working. Powell was a genius at murder. A certifiable psychotic, but also a genius. He set things up beautifully. First of all, the frame couldn't have been neater. He very carefully set up Donahue with means, motive and opportunity. Then he shot the girl and left Donahue on the hook."

I worked on the cognac. "The neat thing was this—if Donahue managed to have an alibi, if by some chance somebody was watching him when the shot was fired, Powell was still in the clear. He himself was one of the few men in the room with no conceivable motive for wanting Karen Price dead."

Ceil moved a little closer on the couch. I put an arm around her. "Then the way he got rid of Donahue was sheer perfection," I continued. "He made it look enough like suicide to close the case as far as the police were concerned. And Jerry Gunther isn't an easy man to bulldoze. He's thorough. But Powell made it look good."

"You didn't swallow it."

"That's because I play hunches. Even so, I was up a tree by then. Because the murder had a double edge to it. Even if he muffed it somehow, even if it didn't go over as suicide, Donahue would be dead and he would be in the clear. Because there was only one way to interpret it—Donahue had been killed by the man who killed Karen Price, obviously, and had been killed so that the original killing would go unsolved. That made me suspect Joe Conn and never let me guess at Powell, not even on speculation. Even with the second killing he hid the fact that Donahue and not Karen was the real target."

"And that's where I came in," she said happily.

"That's exactly where you came in," I agreed. "You and your active imagination. You thought how grim it would be if Karen had only been playing a joke with those phone calls. And that was the only explanation in the world for the calls. I had to believe Donahue was getting the calls, and that Karen was making them. A disguised voice might work once, but she'd called him a few times.

"That left two possibilities, really. She could be jealous—which seemed contrary to everything I had learned about her. Or it could be a gag. But if she was jealous, then why in hell would she take the job popping out of the cake? So it had to be a gag, and once it was a gag, I had to guess why someone would put her up to it. And from that point—"

"It was easy."

"Uh-huh. It was easy."

She snuggled closer. I liked her perfume. Liked the feel of her body beside me.

"It wasn't that easy," she said. "You know what? I think you're a hell of a good detective. And you know what else?"

"What?"

"I also think you're a rotten businessman."

I smiled. "Why?"

"Because you did all that work and didn't make a dime out of it. You got a retainer from Donahue, but that didn't even cover all the time you spent *before* Karen was killed, let alone the time since then. And you probably will never collect."

"I'm satisfied."

"Because justice has been done?"

"Partly. Also because I'll be rewarded."

She upped her eyebrows. "How? You won't make another nickel out of the case, will you?"

"No."

"Then—"

"I'll make something more important than money."

"What?"

She was soft and warm beside me. And it was our third evening together. Not even an amateur tramp could mind a pass on a third date.

"What are you going to make?" she asked, innocently.

I took her face between my hands and kissed her. She closed her eyes and purred like a happy cat.

"You," I said.

Don't Let the Mystery End Here.
Try These Other Great Books From
HARD CASE CRIME!

Hard Case Crime brings you gripping, award-winning crime fiction
by best-selling authors and the hottest new writers in the field.
Find out what you've been missing:

Grifter's Game
by LAWRENCE BLOCK

Con man Joe Marlin was used to scoring easy cash off beautiful
women. But that was before he met Mona Brassard and found
himself facing the most dangerous con of his career, one that
will leave him either a killer—*or a corpse.*

RAVES FOR THE WORK OF
LAWRENCE BLOCK

"Block grabs you…and never lets go."
— Elmore Leonard

"The reader is riveted to the words, the action."
— Robert Ludlum

*"Marvelous…will hold readers
gaga with suspense."*
— New York Newsday

*"He is simply the best at what he does…
If you haven't read him before, you've
wasted a lot of time. Begin now."*
— Mostly Murder

Available now at your favorite bookstore.
For more information, visit
www.HardCaseCrime.com

**A Twisted Tale From
An MWA Grandmaster!**

A Diet of
TREACLE

by LAWRENCE BLOCK

SEX, DRUGS, AND MURDER IN
THE LAND OF THE LOTUS EATERS

Anita Carbone was a good girl—and it bored her.

That's why she took the long subway ride down to Greenwich Village, home of the Beats and the stoners, home to every kind of misfit and dropout and free spirit you could imagine. It was where she met Joe Milani, the troubled young war veteran with the gentle touch. But it was also where she met his drug-dealing roommate—a man whose unnatural appetites led to murder…

THE CRITICS PRAISE
LAWRENCE BLOCK

*"Exceptional…
A whale of a knockout punch to the solar plexus."*
— New York Daily News

"Block knows how to pace a story and tighten the noose of suspense. He…knows his mean streets."
— San Francisco Examiner

*"Lawrence Block is finally getting
the attention he deserved."*
— Chicago Tribune

Available now at your favorite bookstore.
For more information, visit
www.HardCaseCrime.com